SINS OF THE FATHERS

CHRIS LYNCH

HarperTempest

An Imprint of HarperCollins*Publishers*

HARPERTEMPEST IS AN IMPRINT OF HARPERCOLLINS PUBLISHERS.

Sins of the Fathers

Copyright © 2006 by Chris Lynch

www.harperteen.com

Library of Congress Cataloging-in-Publication Data

Lynch, Chris.

Sins of the Fathers / by Chris Lynch.—1st ed.

p.   cm.

Summary: At Boston's Blessed Sacrament Catholic School, Drew, aided by a priest who is far from perfect—and on the wrong side of the Monsignor—stands by his best friends as one struggles to avoid being sent to public school and the other tries to hide serious problems.

ISBN-10: 0-06-074037-X (trade bdg.)

ISBN-13: 978-0-06-074037-5 (trade bdg.)

ISBN-10: 0-06-074038-8 (lib. bdg.)

ISBN-13: 978-0-06-074038-2 (lib. bdg.)

[1. Best friends—Fiction.   2. Friendship—Fiction.   3. Priests—Fiction. 4. Catholic schools—Fiction.   5. Schools—Fiction.   6. Boston (Mass.)—History—20th century—Fiction.]   I. Title.

PZ7.L979739Sin 2006   2006000357

[Fic]—dc22   CIP

AC

Typography by Kristina Albertson

1 2 3 4 5 6 7 8 9 10

First Edition

SINS OF THE FATHERS

PRODIGAL SONS

AT SIX-FIFTEEN ON A BORDERLINE BLIZZARD MORNING, outside my bedroom window, Skitz Fitzsimmons reared his ugly head. I was preoccupied and groggy at the same time, so I didn't even notice him there until he was staring back at me like a lunatic mirror reflection. He had one eye squinted and the other eye wide and his mouth was pinched up in a pucker and shifted way over to the side. Like he always looked.

"So, what's the news? Anything mental in the news today?" he said through the glass of the storm window and the glass of the regular window, all excited, with a big band of snow crust sitting like a ledge on his brow.

"Don't you have a hat?" I asked. He should have

had a hat. Any normal person would have had a hat out there. It was wicked weather.

"Shuddup, who cares about a hat. I don't need a hat. What's mental in the news today?"

"Shuddup, who cares about the news, I'm trying to listen to the no-school report."

It is a magical thing to listen to, the no-school report early in the morning. So early in the morning, and so early in the season. A November storm was magic on top of magic, and because of my working hours, because of my route, I got to listen in on WBZ probably before anybody else was even aware that it was snowing. And it was like a church service, all quiet except for the radio guy chanting the names of towns and of schools I would otherwise never hear in my life except during the no-school reports. Like St. Columbkille's, like the Beaver Country Day School, like the town of Dracut. They might have been names the radio guy made up to keep himself amused early on snowy mornings, but they came to be like old friends when I heard them, because I only heard them on snow days and then they were gone again like chimney smoke.

"C'mon, *newsboy*, deliver the news," Skitz blurted

despite what I told him about shuddup. As a rule, Skitz always blurted, no matter what you told him about shuddup.

"What did I tell you about shuddup?" I said, trying to catch the announcer setting the lucky Ws free. *Waltham, no school all schools. Wellesley, no school all schools. Winthrop . . .*

"Newsboy!" he snapped, boldly.

I looked at him closely, though the window was snowing up on his side and fogging up on mine. He was awfully excited, the way a strange dog can be excited and either follow you home or chew your hands off.

"You want a smack?"

"I don't care," he said, and he didn't, and I knew he didn't before I asked.

"Nobody cares about the news at six-fifteen but you, Skitz, and right now nobody cares about it less than I do because I want to hear the no-schools to see if we got no school, so shuddup."

They were back to the beginning again. *Abington, no school all schools. Acton, no school all schools. Andover, no school all schools . . .*

They were killing me with this. They always killed

me with this. Boston public schools, no school all schools was all they needed to say way up there early in the *B*s, but would they say it? Like hell. They always waited, even if it was obvious, they always waited for three, four whole circuits of the Massachusetts alphabet before the Boston public schools would announce, because Boston had to be the belle of the ball, the Queen of the May, fashionably late so she had everybody's attention. Are the neighborhoods of Boston really more special than, say, Norwell or Northborough, Stow or Williamsburg? Okay, they are, but still there was no excuse.

Skitz, it had to be said, was being awfully good now. He was waiting outside that window just good as gold, framed frozen outside my window like a picture. A picture of a snow-crusted nutball.

And we aren't even Boston public school. God, no, we're *private* school, we're *parochial* school, we're *Catholic* school, which they reminded us every couple of minutes, but since it probably cost a buck or so to get your own separate listing on the no-schools report, we just tagged along with the decision of the Boston public schools and prayed that they came up with some good Catholic judgment at the right time. The diocese didn't have money to splash around capriciously, after all. Which was another something they yapped at us every chance.

I had similar problems myself, and if I didn't get my butt out delivering papers soon, my business was going to suffer. So it was down-to-the-wire, boots-on, hat-on time when the word finally came. *Boston public schools, no school all schools.*

I kissed my clock radio, gave Skitz the two-finger sign that was peace or victory or whatever but right now was *no school all schools,* and his big ugly head disappeared as he threw himself down backward into the snow with joy.

He was still there, on his back, when I got out to the porch.

"You're the ugliest snow angel I ever saw, Skitz."

"Ya," he said.

He stayed there.

"If you don't swing your arms and legs a little bit, there's no angel-action at all, you know. Just makes you a snow-doofus."

"Ya," he said. He still stayed there.

"Threw yourself down too hard, didn't you."

"Ya," he said.

I came down the two steps, past my stack of papers, and curled around to the spot beside the porch, beneath my window, where he lay looking up at me, his close-cropped hatless head embedded in the snow.

"You're mental, Skitz," I said as I crouched by his head and lifted him by his shoulders.

"Duh," he said.

I brushed him off, brushed off his head. "So, you're coming with me on my route?"

Being off the frozen ground seemed to loosen his brain already. "Of course I am. What else am I gonna do?"

"You're gonna put my hat on, is what you're gonna do. How long you been out already?"

"I don't need your hat. I'm not even cold."

"No brain, no pain. How long you been out already?"

"A while," he said. He was shivering slightly, which meant he was fighting it mightily.

"I think it's been more than a while."

"Maybe a while-and-a-half."

I skimmed my hat off my head—I am renowned for this hat, my black Boston Bruins hat with the spoked *B* emblem—and I jammed it down over Skitz's head. He made a protest face, and moved his hands a little like to fight it, but I held that hat there tight over his ears for several seconds. Then when it seemed safe, I let go, but I stuck my finger in his face, as if to say something stern.

I didn't say anything stern. I just gave him the pointy finger. We could have had the words, the old back-and-forth words back and forth to nowhere, but pointing the finger in just the right way could usually cover it. It did. His perfectly oval head looked almost exactly the same with the hat on or off.

"What's in the paper?" he asked, bouncing from one foot to the other for warmth, kicking the steps, hopping up and down.

I had just gotten back up to the porch, pulled my wire cutters out of my pocket. My papers came bundled tight in a wire as thick as a coat hanger, and I had to cut them apart to get at them. "You see my wire cutters? Have I cut the papers open yet? Have I seen the papers yet? I deliver the things, I don't write 'em."

"Ya, what's in there?" he asked again.

I shook my head and cut open the stack and handed him one to shut him up. He pored over that front section while I went right to the back. I did not care about *the news*. There were far more important things in this world.

"Stupid Bruins," I snapped. "Stupid, stupid, stupid Bruins. How do you lose to a team that doesn't even have winter? Can you tell me that? This is the kind of thing that has kept them from winning the Stanley Cup for over thirty years. I don't know why I bother sometimes, I really don't. The *Patriots* are champions, the *Red Sox*, for cryin' out loud, are champions, and still the Bruins aren't humiliated enough to win."

"Listen to this, Drew," Skitz said with deadly seriousness. "See, I knew something was wrong with the fabric of the universe. One of Franklin Park's lion brothers died. He's really dead."

"Who cares? The Bruins are dead, and that's what matters. The fabric of the universe is the same as always, it's the fabric of your brain that's unraveling."

"That shouldn't happen," he said, all blue. "He wasn't even very old. Now his brother is over there all alone and he's pacing around and not eating. That's very sad."

That was pretty much how the conversation continued—that is, we talked to ourselves—while I went about the business of being a paperboy. I counted out the papers—thirty-two *Globe*s and five *Herald*s, just like it was supposed to be. I rolled each one, tucked one end into the other real tight so there'd be no fly-aparts when I threw them, then worked the whole lot into my heavy canvas *Boston Globe* bag with the barely padded orange shoulder strap. The snow blowing onto the porch was fat but light, and didn't bother the papers hardly at all once I got them in the bag.

"Do you need this one?" Skitz asked, offering back the one I gave him.

"Keep it," I said. "Half the people don't expect to get their papers on snow days anyway."

He smiled big, tucked the paper up under his thin jacket, under his shirt, flat against his body like insulation. Then he shoved my hat back down onto my head.

"I'm warm now," he said. "Let's us go to work."

And he meant it. Well, of course he meant it, since Skitz Fitzsimmons is constitutionally incapable of saying what he does not mean. Even when you can't understand him, you're forced to believe him. He went the whole winter with not much for shoes on, and a windbreaker that didn't break anything stronger than a puff, but he was hardly ever cold. I had on my big black rubber boots with the buckles, which slipped up over my shoes and flopped and made sounds like flat tires when I walked. I had on hat and gloves and heavy jacket, and if anybody saw him helping me deliver papers like this they would assume he was some kind of prisoner in my slave-labor camp.

Though you almost couldn't call what he did helping me, since he came pretty close to doing all the work. He was like a hunting dog, running circles around me, barking away, waiting on my orders. There, Skitz, take that *Globe* around to the back, they like me to leave it in the greenhouse when the weather's bad. Good boy, Skitz. Now take this one up and stick it inside the storm door. He was tireless. Tireless two ways, actually. He never got tired. And he didn't have any tires. He skidded and scrabbled his way all over the place, fighting the snow slickness with only his sneakers on. He always only had his sneakers on, unless he had his black cordovan school shoes on, and either way he was in constant jeopardy making his way through snow or ice.

As a team, though, we did the business. I threw the papers I could throw, Skitz escorted all the special deliveries, and we dusted the whole thing off in less time than I ordinarily took in even the best weather.

So it was pretty early yet when we came up to the big place. Early enough that it was still dark, though we didn't expect to find a light on in the reptile house.

We stood there for a minute, staring at the house, the rectory. It was a hulking impressive oppressive thing with two big windows on either side of the porch, a row of five more straight across the second floor, and three more dormers sprouting out of the roof. The clapboards were painted a thick forest green, and the bright white shutters all had shamrock holes carved out of them. It was no revelation or anything to find it here, since I found it here every morning. But it felt different now, looked different, with somebody else here, with Skitz here. It looked darker, it looked bigger, and it looked more alert.

"They like the paper put into the mailbox inside the

storm door," I said, pushing the rolled-up paper at him.

"No way in hell," Skitz said in a voice so low and cold it made me shiver in a way the snowstorm did not.

We both stared for a few seconds more, both drifting gazes toward the brand-fresh-new tire tracks in the snow in the driveway. Your eye had to follow that line, up the drive, along to the porch, in, upstairs, and into that room on the second-floor front with the light burning bright.

They were very fresh tracks. New snow hadn't even had the chance to build up in them. He had just gotten home before we got there. Father had a soft spot for single-parent, free-cheese-program families and was always out there helping them out, God bless him.

It was rare for Father to spend the whole night. It had to be special people or a special occasion. Maybe snow was a special occasion.

"Ah, the Prodigal Son has returned to his home," Skitz hissed. "I guess that means I can return to mine."

The Prodigal Son. That was our religious and theatrical point of reference, no matter what the situation. Didn't matter whether it made sense under the circumstances or not, if there was a return involved, or a son . . . or a departure, or a father, or any movement whatsoever toward something or away from it. We whipped out the old Prodigal Son book of remarks. Sense didn't matter because we knew what we meant. That was us, Skitz and me, onstage in fourth grade, right there in the church in front of everyone for our big First Penance performance, the centerpiece of the whole ceremony. Skitz played, as you'd figure, the wayward son who ran off and had all the laughs and the Playboy bunnies and the racing cars and Dad threw him a party when he came home again, just for coming home again. I played the loser son who stayed home all along and did all the good-boy grunt work and got a big squat sandwich for his troubles. Chump.

We were supposed to have learned something from it. Smack me if I knew what. Our reviews were very good, however.

"Don't go yet," I said to him as he stood staring at the window. "Just let me ram his paper in his mailbox and I'll walk you home."

Skitz stood there quiet like a good boy while I trudged up the steps to the rectory, slogged across the vast expanse of front porch, and wedged the paper tightly into the cozy warm nook between the inside door and the outside.

I was pushing them back together, listening to the vacuum *whoosh* of perfectly weather-stripped doors sucking away air, when the smash of glass shattered everything else around us.

I knew, of course. I couldn't believe it, but I knew it, before I even looked.

Skitz was hightailing it, wheeling his arms more than his legs as he tried to keep his feet under him rounding the corner. I skittered back across the porch, tipping the quickest, most unnecessary glance over my shoulder as I ran. I didn't need to look, but how could you not look, and I saw the big spider of a hole in that second-floor window and I saw the black shadow, the backlit figure just standing there behind the curtain not doing anything, not saying anything, not missing anything as I ski-jumped over the five front steps and skidded away behind the snowy moguls of parked cars.

LIKE
NOBODY'S PRIEST

"HOW COME, WHEN THEY BECOME CARDINALS, 'CARDINAL' becomes their middle name? And if it's a real name, an acceptable Christian name, can I pick it for my confirmation name? That would be cool."

Skitz Cardinal Fitzsimmons. Maybe not.

"Humberto. There used to be a cardinal named Humberto here. Now *that* would be cool, to take a cardinal's own name for a confirmation name. I think he'd be very impressed. Might even invite me to the big cardinal house for supper."

Hector Humberto Fossas. Could work.

"You take Humberto, I'll take Cardinal, and we'll see who he takes home with him."

"He'll probably take both of you," I said. "He is a cardinal, after all."

"Hey, watch it," Hector Protector said.

I didn't mean it. Everybody thought the cardinal was all right. And if he wanted to bring somebody home to the big house on the big day, certainly he'd pick Hector, an equally good egg and one of the best friends Jesus H. ever had.

We were supposed to be singing. We were getting ready for our Confirmation, which was going to happen later in the year, around Easter time. So they were using up two of our Wednesday afternoons every month making us learn all the really important stuff that would make us permanent indelible Catholicos for the rest of our natural lives and beyond, and right now we were supposed to be singing this song, but no kidding, how could you?

> *Sons of God*
> *Hear His Holy Word*
> *Gather round the*
> *Table of the Lord,*
> *Eat His body*

Drink His blood
And we'll sing a
Song of love. . . .

All right?

"Am I wrong, or does this song make us sound like a tribe of ghouls?"

I was asking Skitz and Hector, but I was asking too loudly. I caught Father's attention. It wasn't something you'd really want to catch.

Father wanted to know if I had a problem. I wanted to know if Father had a problem, but I didn't get to ask. He got to ask me, though.

"No, Father, I don't got a problem."

Father said I did have a problem. He said I had a grammatical problem, which I didn't, I just talk how I'm comfortable, but that was not my problem of the moment. Sing, he said, was my problem of the moment, so I sang a couple of lines of the zombie song and then got back to where I was in my conversation.

"It's like something out of a wicked bad horror movie that's only scary because the dumb little freaks keep singing along like it's *The Sound of Music* instead of blood drinkin' and body eatin'. We have to be out of our minds here. No way does the rest of the world know what we're up to, or else they would be here pounding down the doors, with flaming torches and pointed sticks and stuff. What's the difference between us and pagan devil worshippers who eat babies and sacrifice virgins and live in caves and marry goats? We're pretty much the same, if you go by our music and all. Except I would *bet* there's not one other major religion that eats its own actual God."

"Would you shuddup? Would you? Just for a while?" Hector wanted me to shuddup for a while. He could be very Catholic sometimes, but he was still a good guy. The ghoul.

It was a great church, though, the building anyway. I'd stack it against anybody's. A fine building to spend your Wednesday afternoons in, or your Sunday mornings, or even your Holy Days of Obligation. It never felt to me like an obligation, to be forced to sit in Blessed Sacrament Church, because Blessed Sacrament Church was a great old place, full of great old stuff, gold and purple and burgundy embroidered images of saints and massive crucifixes that gave me a chill when nobody else was there with me or when Skitz actually was. Full of history, Jesus' history and my history and my family's history, with weddings and deaths and baptisms going back about twelve generations before the *Mayflower* landed just down the road a bit and to the left. And it was a warm place, in spite of its hugeness and the fact that there was always bellyaching about how there was no money to fix the bleeding roof or fire the gigantic furnace and so I had to cough up for a *second* collection instead of getting that peanut butter cup I had been drooling over since I had to skip breakfast because I had to run to make Mass.

No, the place was great. I think I could even have lived in this place, which would have been impossibly slick, though a little bit eerie.

It was the Franchise. The operation in charge is what tended to muck things up.

That would be the firm of Fathers Blarney, Mullarkey, and Shenanigan, and whatever you might think of their names, those were their names. Though sometimes names are changed to protect the innocent, like on cop shows, but unlike on cop shows the innocent here is me. Oh, and Father Blarney is a monsignor and you'd damn well better call him that if he was in earshot. What is a monsignor? I didn't know, and I'd bet he didn't either other than it gave him the right to be bossy and mean as hell and march around like he was pissed off at everybody all the time. And he had very white thick hair and a red thick face, making him look more seriously alarmed, not to mention alarming.

But Monsignor Blarney was still a Father, like Father Mullarkey and Father Shenanigan. Kind of a shell game, really, you could switch them all around *whish-whoosh-whish*, and then back around *whoosh-whish-whish*, and while you thought you had followed closely enough and you thought you could identify which was which because they looked different from each other, you picked your pick and underneath you still found the same thing underneath. Priest.

It was stacked. House always wins, so don't play. House always wins.

And this was unquestionably Father's house.

"Who was with you at my house yesterday morning?" Father Shenanigan wanted to know. He was looming over me, all eight feet eleven of him, with his swoopy black wingspan of a mustache spreading out both ways off him like the big awful condor face that he was.

"Nobody, Father."

He had caught me on my way into school. When you enter the grounds you pass the rectory first, then the church on the way toward the rest of the buildings in the compound. Even when you couldn't see anybody you couldn't pass that way without the heavy feeling you were passing through God's tollbooth, or his customs department with his goons watching to grab you. *Bang bang bang*, he grabbed me too. He was hulking there in the side door of the church, the clear glass door looking like a big horrible stained-glass window of himself. He beckoned me inside.

"Did you break my window, Andrew?"

"No, Father. I'm your paperboy, Father."

"That's right. It would be stupid for my paperboy to break my window at exactly the time he was delivering my paper. And you're not stupid, are you, Andrew?"

"No, Father, I don't think I am."

"Nor crazy. You are neither stupid nor crazy, are you?"

"No, I'm not."

"No, you're not. But who is? Who would be stupid or crazy enough to break my window?"

"He didn't do it, Father."

"So who did, then? Don't lie. Lying's a sin. A confessable sin you will have to bring to the confessional."

"I have no idea, Father."

"Stop calling me that," he snapped. "I don't like the way you say that. Stop it."

"Sorry, Father."

Whaddya think, did I get a smack for that? Would you have smacked me? I probably would have smacked me. No, I definitely would have smacked me.

But that didn't make it right.

When the year started, back in September, there were only the two of them, Shenanigan and Blarney. We still felt outgunned, but at least it was only the two of them, and if they asked us we would not have kicked and screamed to add a new guy. Maybe if we had kicked and screamed for one he never would have shown up at all. But we didn't and he did, and there you go.

Sister told us we were having a *special guest*. Because we were older now, and edging closer to being out in the real world, Sister was frequently producing *special guests* to come in and enlighten us with their wisdom. One of them was a retired teacher who came and sedated us with slides of her pilgrimages to both Lourdes *and* Fatima. The moral of the story being, for God's sake don't ever retire. Another of them was the guy who worked third shift at the central nursery for the whole city, making sure the flowers in all ten green-houses were watered and guarded through the night so that our parks and civic events could be alive with color. The moral of the story being, for God's sake don't ever work. There were a bunch more *special guests*, but they all pretty much fell into one or the other of those two morals.

But they were usually on time. This one was late, and that presented a problem for Sister who, bless her, could not sing without a hymn sheet. If Sister didn't have a carefully detailed plan for each and every moment of the day, a plan she had slaved over the whole night before while everybody else was squandering his life away on life, then she was adrift. And she had planned her morning around our *special, late guest*.

So we were treated to our favorite, rare instruction: "You may talk quietly amongst yourselves for now."

"How long, exactly, does a fart hang in the air after you leave it?" Skitz asked instantly.

I turned to my right to face him, and it overwhelmed me. I was about to complain but feared exposing my open mouth to it.

Hector took over. From one row farther away, he was outside the death circle but still well within the deeply offended area. "Cripes, Skitz."

"It's reached there already, then," Skitz said. "So, how long does it hang in the air altogether?"

"How long you gonna hang in the air after I kick you to the ceiling, ya disgusting pig?"

"I don't think I'd hang as long as this fart," Skitz said with a combination of pride and scientific seriousness.

The toxicity had some effect on Hector's reasoning. "Well, get rid of it, right now."

Skitz spluttered out laughing.

"Oh ya?" Hector said, "If you don't, I'm gonna fink that you broke the rectory window."

Skitz's face melted down into a glare, which isn't the

most intimidating thing. "Shuddup, Hector. I mean it. Shuddup."

One of Hector's only nicknames that didn't rhyme with Hector was "The Carpetfitter," because when he walked he looked like he had a two-hundred-pound rug rolled up under each arm, and he looked like he would have no trouble carrying them. There weren't a lot of people who told Hector to shuddup. But there weren't a lot of Skitz Fitzsimmonses either. They represented kind of the far reaches of the Catholic thing too. Skitz was just along for the ride mostly, but Hector came from one of those very serious families who believed the Church was everything and everything they said was true no matter how sci-fi it sounded. He didn't believe it was everything, exactly, but he believed it was right up there. He somehow managed to be all right anyway.

"I don't believe you will tell me shuddup again," Hector said calmly.

"I do believe I am telling you shuddup right now," Skitz said.

They really are good friends. It's just that a lot of the time it's a good thing that they have me in between them. I have fine interpersonal skills.

"All right, guys," I said. "Listen, Hector's not telling anybody anything about the window, and Skitz, in return, will stop being rancid. There."

"There," Skitz said, smiling. "Shake on it."

It transpired right across my desk, right in my face. Skitz extended his hand in the traditional gesture of friendship and deal making. Hector at first looked at the hand as if Skitz had just pulled it out of his underwear. Then he relented. But just as the shake almost happened, Skitz curled back all the fingers, except one.

"Oh jeez," I said, "why do you have to ruin everything, Skitz? Forget it, nobody is pulling that finger."

"No," Hector said, and I turned to see him smiling, but not smiling. His face was red and intense. You could hear the breath whistling through his bared teeth.

See, that's the kind of signal most people would see, but Skitz somehow always misses.

Hector reached out, grabbed the finger, and ripped.

I saw, right up close in front of my eyeballs, as the finger came clearly and awkwardly out of its socket.

I squirmed and pulled away. Hector, shocked at what he'd done, gasped.

Skitz had a bit of a grimace on his face but didn't say anything more than a kind of a "huh" that seemed like he found it more curious than painful. The other sound he made—like hooking a goose up to the PA system and then jumping on it—was far more noteworthy.

Which was right about when the *special guest* came in.

"Jesus, who did *that*?" he asked out loud. Very loud.

"I'm sorry, Father Mullarkey," Sister said. Sorry for what, she probably didn't know.

"So it was you then, Sister," Father said.

Despite the air quality in the room, every mouth dropped open. Sister's included. Already, he was something we had never encountered before.

"No," Sister said, pleadingly. "No, it was not. . . ."

"I know, Sister," he said. "I'm sorry, I was just kidding." He put an arm around her shoulders and escorted her to the door. Sister was normally about the midrange on the sisterly scale of might: she was not routinely abusive or unfair, but she was hardly a marshmallow either. Priests, man. They turned them all buttery.

He closed the door, and the room was now officially

his, and he was officially ours. We could hardly believe it. *This* was our new priest? This was like nobody's priest.

In addition to his eye-catching entrance, he was a whole eyeful himself. He was a revelation. He was a whole Book of Revelations. We had never seen a Father like Father Mullarkey, and I'd bet nobody else had either. First, he dressed like a free-walking citizen rather than a priest. A big fan of denim, of ripped denim and patches and T-shirts that looked like he was spray-painted with a hose.

What else he was very much like was a Hells Angels motorcycle club guy, which meant he looked like a big meat-eating hippie with long hair, an acre of ginger beard, and strappy, bumpy muscles. He looked like a hippie that ate hippies. He sounded like a talking bear.

"Right now," he said, clapping his hands, "now that the air is clear . . ."

He strode across the front of the room and back again, getting a good look. Then suddenly he homed in, like catching the scent of something scared and delicious. He came right down my way.

"What gives?" Father asked.

It was Skitz. He was sitting there mesmerized, his elbow on the desk, investigating his own dislocated finger.

Skitz just looked up at him and shrugged.

Everybody saw it now. Everybody hit the same groan-pitch.

Hector squirmed like a guilty man.

"That's quite something," Father said, touching the finger lightly, looking at it from all angles. "Are you not in pain?"

Skitz shrugged. "A little?" Like he had to guess what the right answer was.

"How long has it been like this?"

"Coupla minutes?"

"Coupla . . . ? You mean this happened here? Sitting at your desk?"

"Guess so."

"Who did it?"

"Nobody, Father. I mean, me. I did it."

Father had his mouth open, his brow furrowed, and was poised to pursue. Then he stopped. Then he smiled, and tapped his temple with his middle finger. "Hold on," he said. "This is good. You know what we have here, students? We have a mystery." He grabbed Skitz by the collar, nicely, and tugged him to the front of the class. "What's your name, son?"

"Skitz, Father."

"I like it. Now, how many people here believe Mister Skitz was capable of dislocating his *own* finger while sitting there quietly at his desk?"

Nearly every hand in the room went up. Even mine, and I knew the truth. Even Hector's, and he *did* it. But Skitz was capable.

Father Mullarkey looked at Skitz quizically, but not without some appreciation. "You must be a pip."

"I am a pip," Skitz said modestly.

"But you didn't do that finger, did you?"

Skitz pursed his lips tight. That was him being a noble, stand-up guy.

"Yes, a mystery," Father said again. "An Agatha Christie mystery, as rewritten by a thirteen-year-old male. Let's work it out." He leaned close to Skitz and made a big exaggerated sniff. "It was you, wasn't it. The smell. It's still clinging to you."

Skitz looked down at his feet. Father lifted his chin back up with one finger.

"Don't be shy," Father said, "that was quality work you did. Just don't do it again." Then he left Skitz to address the rest of us, like a big corny detective. "Right. Now, we all know how a high-octane odor like that gets extracted from a young man, don't we?" He rocked back and forth, toe-to-heel, heel-to-toe. Then he held up his right-hand pointer, and like a conductor, waved up the class with both hands and a "One-two-three. . . ."

"Pull-My-Finger!" we all called out.

"Yes," Father said, suddenly all solemn. "We've all been there. That noxicity can only be produced by the pulling of a finger. Pull my finger, indeed." Slowly he began making his way down the aisle, my aisle, to the scene of the crime. I gulped as he hovered over me. He was one big priest, big all over the place. Then he wedged his big self right down into Skitz's seat.

And what a sensation I had now. A gigantic hairy priest was sitting in the seat next to me with his hands folded, being scary smiley and quiet, I was sweating, suddenly feeling like I was on trial for something, and there up at the front of the class was the image of Skitz Fitzsimmons as the teacher, and he was now wagging his creepy damaged number seven of a finger at us all.

"It was," Father continued, "deeply unpleasant by all accounts. But certainly those most victimized by whatever roadkill Mister Skitz had for breakfast this morning were the people in the immediate vicinity of this spot here. The very people who would be in finger-pulling radius." With that, Father unfurled his arms and stretched them, and stretched them, on and on until he had achieved his whole unnatural reach, extending right past me to the edge of Hector's desk and the same length on the other side.

He looked to his right, two girls. "Morning, ladies," he said. He looked behind, and greeted another likewise.

Then he turned my way. A toothy smile opened up and he said, "Did you know that ninety-seven point seven percent of all finger-pullers are male? Isn't that fascinating?"

I was starting to see an immediate future of broken fingers. That's what they do, you know. Whatever offense you seem to be committing, they give you a taste of the same thing. Like when I was making chop suey out of my handwriting exercises even though I was doing the best I could and Sister came over and whacked my hand crisply with a ruler and I shouted and told her that was hardly going to improve my handwriting. So she said, Well, maybe you should try using *that* one, and whacked the other one even harder. Or when Skitz could not get his sums right when he was working up at the blackboard and she came up from behind and banged his head against the board. Granted, it was Skitz, but nobody's going to get smarter from that.

So as Father got up and cast his great shadow over me and Hector, I was steeling myself.

He held his hands together like praying. I was ready to join him.

"I'm bored with the mystery now," Father announced, winked at me, and spun away toward Skitz. "Did they tell you, class, that I used to be in the circus before I joined the priesthood?"

"I was this close to squirting myself," Hector whispered.

"I think I have drips," I said.

"And not the cheesy circuses you usually see around here, where they put a chimp on a bike and whack an elephant with a broom handle until he stands on one foot. I mean the real European circuses where everybody has a one-of-a-kind skill and the integrity of the freaks is unparalleled. This is what I did. . . ."

We all stared as Father rolled up his sleeve. He revealed a long and muscled, gnarly arm with lots of thick red hair and freckles all over it. He held the arm straight out to the side, palm up, elbow down. Then, gradually, the hand, the wrist, the forearm turned, twisted, flattened again until the palm and the elbow were both facing the floor.

Father then looked around to be sure everybody was looking—like we'd be doing anything else.

"Now I would like my lovely assistant here to come over and touch my arm lightly with that magic finger of his."

"This one?" Skitz asked, producing the finger.

"Yes. Please."

Skitz touched it.

It was like a man dropping from a gallows. Father Mullarkey's arm fell, from the elbow, and dangled lifelessly with the fingers stretching to the floor. His biceps was still visible, straining toward the ceiling.

The elbow was bent backward.

The howls and squeals filled the room. He had actually somehow undone the joint and left it disconnected while he walked along the front row to show the horrified, recoiling kids.

"That was my thing," Father said as he finally stopped. Gently, he bent and stooped, angled and eased the joint back into place. "I can do it with any joint in my body. Now, I am a special case. Under no circumstances is anyone to *ever* try—"

"Father," somebody shouted and pointed behind Father.

Skitz was already at it, using his undamaged hand to try and dislodge the elbow of his other arm.

"Not under any circumstances," Father said, grabbing Skitz by both shoulders. He took Skitz's hand then. "Would you like me to put this finger back right for you?" he asked.

"Really?" Skitz sounded like it would be an honor.

"You trust me, you wouldn't rather go to a doctor?" Father asked.

"Duh, Father, of course I trust you. Look at all the cool stuff you can do."

"Righto," he said, and cuffed his hands over Skitz's finger, did a little pulling, a little squeezing, a little massaging, then a quick snap. "There. Did that hurt?"

Skitz was taking the finger for a test drive, wiggling, jabbing, scratching himself. "I dunno," he said.

At that point Sister eased back into the room, first appearing as a floating head in the crack of the door. She was concerned, as you would be, to find Skitz at the head of the class, playing with his finger.

"Oh no, what has he done now, Father?" she asked.

"Not a thing, Sister," he said, waving Skitz back to his seat. "In fact, he was an invaluable assistant as I displayed some of the digital manipulation I gained in my circus career."

"Oh," she said, still a floating head. And the head didn't look any more relieved by the circus thing.

"Come on in, Sister," Father Mullarkey said. "I didn't realize how much of your class time I was taking up. We were having such a good time."

She came in, walked up beside him, and stood there as if they were going to sing a duet. Then he draped a big jolly arm over her shoulders. Her knees buckled slightly under the weight of it.

"Oh my," she said. Everyone giggled. "Well, oh . . ." Sister was not used to physical contact unless it was initiated by her, and the contact was limited to the palm of her hand and the top of your head. Praise or punishment, that was the way it went. "Have we all gotten to know Father Mullarkey well now?"

"Not as well as you're doing," Skitz called out.

Father laughed a big belly laugh. Everybody laughed.

Well, not everyone. "I'll see you after class, Mr. Fitzsimmons."

And because my pal Skitz can never dig a hole deep enough . . .

"Okay, Sister, but I'm afraid you're gonna be disappointed, after the big guy."

Father Mullarkey was actually required to hold her back, I could see as she leaned our way and he squeezed her shoulders tightly, warmly. With his free hand he pointed at Skitz. "Hey. Show respect," he said. Somehow he managed to get the important part of the job done—I nodded, and he wasn't even talking to me—while at the same time winking his appreciation.

Sister got herself composed. "Before Father has to go, would anyone like to ask him any questions?"

Skitz raised his hand.

"Would anyone," she elaborated, "who is not banned from speaking like to ask a question?"

Manus "The Organ" Morgan: "Were you a for-real carney, and if so, did you ever kill anybody?"

Father Mullarkey: "No, I was not a carney. I was part of a long and distinguished tradition of skilled circus artistes."

Organ: "Right. Sorry, Father. Then you didn't kill anybody."

Father. "Sure, I killed a couple of guys. But that was in the priesthood, not the circus. Next?"

Maria Magdalena Cruz, aka "Knuckles": "Since the Bible says God created man in his own image, do we have to believe that image is not a woman, and if we don't believe it, is that a sin?"

Father's eyes went wide, while Sister's practically squinted shut. She slipped out of Father's grip and took her seat at her desk, from where she could make faces and scowl us out of asking *unhelpful* questions. That was her favorite term for anything that wanted to make her scream, *unhelpful*. As in, "Mr. Fitzsimmons, that was unhelpful of you to expose your bottom in the school bus window," or, "Mr. Fitzsimmons, that was the most unhelpful thing any Christian has ever written on an emergency exit door," or, "Mr. Fitzsimmons. . . ."

Father Mullarkey: "I guess you don't want to know what my favorite color or baseball team is, huh?"

Knuckles: "Not really, Father."

Father: "Good. My answer on the God's-own-image question is, it's not a sin. You have to question."

Sister gasped, and quickly covered her mouth with her hands trying to stuff it back in.

Father turned around to her and shrugged, then turned back to us. "That's the educational tradition I come from. I was taught to question. Look, I can't tell you with a straight face that God looks like me. Lucky guy if he does, but maybe not. For all I can work out, God's *image* might be less like me and more like you, young lady, or like Sister. Or why not a star, or a crayfish, or a fungus? Or a breeze, or a tone, or something I have never even contemplated?"

There was a good several seconds' silence.

Maya DiGregorio, also known as Knuckles: "You

can do that? You can just go around thinking whatever you want?"

Father: "I'm a Jesuit. I can do anything."

Weirdly, Sister started clapping then as she bounded up out of her seat and scurried to Father's side. It felt less like adulation, though, than an act getting the hook.

"Thank you, Father, thank you very much," Sister said nervously, almost touching Father with a hand on his back, but just catching herself and miming the action instead. "Wouldn't we all like to thank Father Mullarkey?" she said in a rather commanding-sounding question. We clapped a little, muttered sloppy thanks, then clapped some more. It was building, I think, as the whole thing set in and we realized better what had just happened, who this guy was, and how much we might actually like this priest.

This was like nobody's priest.

"By the way," he said as he was getting broomed out, "despite the fact that I actually grew up not far from here, my favorite baseball team is the Oakland A's though I prefer Bruins hockey, and my favorite color is anything but black. Thanks for having me, see you again soon. . . ." And he was out the door.

When he was gone, Sister closed the door crisply behind him and leaned with her back and all her weight against it.

"Firstly," she said, "God doesn't look anything like me. . . ."

STEM TO STERN

EVERYONE JOKED ABOUT PRIESTS BEING FENDER BENDERS.
It didn't have to mean anything, just talk. You never
heard a story direct, from *the guy* himself who learned
about it the hard way, but instead you got it from the
guy who heard it from the guy who heard about it from
a pretty good friend of *the guy*, so you never felt completely like believing it or not believing it. Felt like saying it though, anyway.

Or not everyone. Hector Fossas never really felt
like making that kind of joke. His Catholicism got in
the way. But he liked doing lots of other things that
made up for it, in terms of friendworthiness. Like,
he'd play street hockey with you in a blizzard, at no

notice, with no stick, with a broken leg. Like, he'd keep you from taking a beating. I know that for a fact because he stopped me taking a beating on three separate occasions, one of them being from himself when he just got tired and stopped punching me, but the other two were serious and cost him some personal blood but he didn't care. If somebody was punching me or even Skitz and that person was not Hector, Hector took it like it was himself in pain and you could just about see tears in his eyes, before he made the other guy cry. And long after we all got too big to exchange Christmas cards or birthday presents, Hector was still at it, leaving something in your desk when you weren't noticing so you wouldn't be embarrassed, because he wasn't embarrassed at all. I got a blue bottle of aftershave for turning twelve, even though I didn't shave but he did. "You're way ahead of me on this," I said, finding the bottle, rubbing my smooth cheek, blushing. "I'll wait up for you," he said, scratching his own rough mug.

He was always waiting up for me when I fell behind. And I knew he always would.

◆   ◆   ◆

"Meditation," Skitz said.

"*What?*" I asked.

"You heard me, Drew. Meditation. Like the yoga people do. That's what I do to keep from going mental."

"Oh," I said. "I got ya. That's meditation, spelled *m-a-s-t-u-r-b*—"

"Shuddup with that again."

"Ya, jeez please, shuddup with that again, Drew," Hector said. "Father said this place needs to be clean, stem to stern, before he gets back."

Skitz's death wish made an appearance here as he told Hector, "I think what he said was that he wants to apply *his* stem to *your* stern."

Oh hell. I mean, good one, but oh hell.

"It was just a joke," Skitz said, backing up, backing up as Hector advanced on him like a tank. His face was reddening, his eyes were reddening, his hands were squeezed into stony-looking fists.

It was just a joke. "It was just a joke," I said, shuffling in between them.

"It was just a joke," Skitz said, running backward as fast as he had ever run forward.

He could be like this, Hector. Not that he didn't

have a sense of humor, but it could take long and unpredictable vacations, and he could be set off by all kinds of things. He was really religious, really Catholic, even though most of the time he wasn't weird about it. On his best days he could even jump in with a good Jesus joke, say about Jesus stinking up the bathroom and his mother going in the bathroom and shouting, "Sweet Jesus, what kind of unholy stench is that!" But he would still bow his head each and every time he said Jesus, which I think about says it about the varieties of Hector. Then, on his less good days, we could get this:

"I'm gonna kill you, Skitz," Hector said. "Ya weasel. How 'bout I apply a stem to *your* stern? How 'bout I attach a hockey stick to your stern, then twist it around a little bit? Funny, huh?"

"No," Skitz said in a desperate whistle-speak. "Not funny. In fact, I bet it would hurt me very much."

"Correct," Hector said, looking left and right, apparently for his hockey stick. He carried it with him a lot, in case a spontaneous street hockey game broke out. It was a stick with a lot of miles on it, the blade had about three rolls of electrical tape holding it together, and instead of being a rigid curve it wobbled around the end of his stick floppy and black as a six-month-old banana. Still, you have to think it would hurt if he did what he was suggesting. A lot.

I was leaning into Hector pretty good, but my feet were still sliding backward over the floor. "It was just a joke," I said in my never-fail soothing-the-savage-beast voice.

Well, sometimes-fail. "Ya? Here's another joke. This weasel-face guy walks out of a church with a hockey stick sticking out his ass . . ."

"Meditate, Hector. . . . Meditation," Skitz said in a voice meant to sound like a chant but which sounded a lot more like a guy almost crying, for very good reason.

"What is happening here?" Father Shenanigan bellowed, ringing the bells with the reverb of his voice.

We were in the open basement of the church. The basement was called St. Gerald's Hall, possibly that was where St. Gerald hung his coat. Lately it was used for functions. We were the three-man crew cleaning St. Gerald's Hall for a function as a punishment for something we were not technically convicted of doing, but nobody ever said the church was a hotbed of human rights. Nobody.

Father Shenanigan thought Skitz broke his window with a snowball the morning of the snowstorm when Skitz came with me on my paper route. And he thought I knew about it because it happened at exactly the moment I was there delivering his newspaper, and because he watched, through the snowball-size hole in his window, as I skittered across his porch and his sidewalk toward the direction of Skitz's house, where someone Skitzish could also be seen running. Circumstantial, but there you go.

Why was Hector there? Because Hector was our friend. Father thinks that's enough, apparently, but there you go.

"Cleaning's going on here, Father," I called back.

"Stem to stern, Father," Skitz called, because Skitz cannot leave well enough alone, because Skitz has no sense of self-preservation.

The only real suspense was which one of them was going to get to Skitz first, and give him the thump. It was kind of lose-lose for Skitz, since Hector was strong as a bison but basically kind, while Father was long and wiry but deeply mean. Getting rapped with Father's tungsten knucklature was most unpleasant, I can tell you.

And the winner was . . . Hector Fossas.

He smacked me aside like an NFL lineman, and Skitz was my unfortunate unprotected quarterback. Then Hector caught him and dumped him on the floor in much the same NFL nasty fashion. It made me wince to feel it through the floor, the thump of Skitz's lifeless-looking chassis crumpling in an unnatural formation of bone and pale meat and baggy school uniform. Then Hector stood over him and kicked him once, medium-hard.

I whipped around to see what kind of fury Father was bringing now, as this kind of slapstick was way off the charts of what was allowed around here unless you were a nun.

He was bringing very little fury, as it turned out. And he was bringing it very slowly. I looked back around to the Hecto-Skitzo conflict, which in truth was not much of a conflict, to find Hector looking surprised as well. He clearly expected to be restrained and possibly incarcerated by now. Finding that he was not, he turned and kicked Skitz once more good in the ribs, forcing the reverse-breath pig-squeal noise out of him.

Then he turned again to wait.

Father had finally arrived at the scene of the crime.

"What's this all about?" he asked without much indication he cared. He swept his hand back over the slick-rich greaseball hair arrangement he was so proud of. His hand came down glistening.

"Nothing, Father," I said quickly.

"Clamp it, St. Cyr. You're the only one who was not involved."

"Nothing, Father," came the weak but plucky voice from the floor.

"You weren't showing much, that's for sure," Father said. Then he turned, turned his attention, his focus, his whole physical presence, to Hector the Aggressor.

"Well?" Father asked Hector from close range.

"It was me, Father," Skitz said, on his feet now and leaning against me. "It was my fault."

"Of course it was, Fitzsimmons, it's always your fault. But that's not the point, is it?"

Skitz believed that was a question. "I kinda thought it kinda was, Father."

"Quiet," snapped Father. Then back to Hector. "The point, Mr. Fossas, as you well know, as we have discussed before, is that we have no violence here. We will tolerate no violence here, Mr. Fossas."

"Sorry, Father," I said, just to cut in really, because this did not feel good, "but it wasn't violence really. It was just Skitz."

"Ya," Skitz said eagerly. "It wasn't violence, 'cause it was just me, so it doesn't count. A victimless crime."

We knew, in the realest sense, we were right. We knew, even realer, we were going to get no place.

Hector couldn't hold back a little smile, at the job we were making of it.

"Funny, Mr. Fossas?" Father said.

That was the end of the discussion. Father simply took hold of Hector's tie and led him like a pack animal across St. Gerald's Hall toward the exit.

"What about us?" Skitz called, because he is mental.

"The two of you are to clean this place, stem to stern, before I get back," Father bellowed.

Skitz opened his unwise mouth to respond, and I quickly clapped my hand over it, hard. But the urge to make his remark was too strong and he tried to fight loose, so I gripped his face harder, and when he still tried to fight me off I squeezed harder again, practically lifted him, and dumped him right back down on the floor.

We both whipped around, expecting Father's return to visit swift justice because we have no violence here.

"Knock it off," Father said, tugging Hector through the exit door, "and get back to work."

Skitz sat in his spot there on the cold floor and stared at the door as it closed. "I don't like it," he said.

"Sorry, but I had to dump you 'cause you wouldn't shuddup."

"I didn't care about that. I don't like the other stuff. What's he hauling Hector away for? It was all of us. And where's he taking him to? Keeping him after school? It's *already* after school. What's he, gonna keep him after-after school? Then he'll keep him till tomorrow?"

"I don't know," I said, picking up my long broom. "He'll be fine. He'll get over it. Everybody gets over it."

"Not me. I'm going to see where he's taking him. I'm following. You coming?"

He started running for the door. I grabbed the tail of his shirt, but he just dragged me along. "No, I'm not coming," I said, "and neither are you."

"Where should we look?" he asked, because from the forward progress we were still making I was apparently going with him whether I thought so or not.

We went out, up the stairs toward the main body of the church. We walked all crouchy and peeky like a couple of lame half-wit World War II movie spies afraid of their own shadows as much as the Nazis. At the top of the stairs we scooted right out the back door to the sprawling courtyard that was the converging point of all the Blessed Sacrament properties—the church, two school buildings, the convent, the string of garages, and the rectory. We went straight across the courtyard to the lower school building where we went for first through fourth grade, which seemed like a hundred thousand years before now. Front door, side door, locked. There was no sign of life. We hustled to the upper school building and found the same.

"Of course, dummy," I said, smacking Skitz for not knowing what we both should have known. "There's nothing in there. The second we leave the building in the afternoon they close everything down, no lights, no heat, no nothing, to save the money. That's why it's like a meat locker when we get there in the morning." I pulled him by the sleeve back toward the church.

"So where is he?" Skitz asked. His short strip of forehead was scrunched almost out of business.

"What does it matter, ya freak. All I know is, *we* still have to clean up the hall by ourselves. Hector probably planned it all out. I bet he got off with a clap across the head and now he's home, but if Father catches us not finishing the work we'll get smacks *and* more work to do."

Skitz didn't respond, but neither did he resist me pulling him back to the job ahead. "Let's just go finish the job so Shenanigan can't have any reason to get at us, and then we'll scram."

We were back inside the glass door now. Just to our right was the stairway to St. Gerald's Hall. Straight ahead we could see all the way to the back of the church. On our left was the altar, a few yards ahead on our right was the door to the sacristy.

"I want to keep looking," Skitz said grimly.

"Sheesh," I said, "when you get a bee in your bonnet, boy . . ."

"I want to look," he said, the same way.

"And I want to work."

He turned and headed down the aisle. "Fine," he said. "Work."

Sometimes, regardless of the circumstances, you just can't leave Skitz Fitzsimmons to do things without proper supervision. A lot of people would argue that you never can.

"Aw, hell," I said, and caught right up behind him.

He was stopped on the two red-carpeted steps that lead up to the sacristy door. His hand was gripped on the carved and madly detailed brass doorknob that we all knew intimately. Polishing the brass around here served chain-gang purposes.

"You know," I whispered, "Hector got himself into trouble by beating you up. You do remember that, don't you?"

"No," he said defiantly, "I don't. He wouldn't let this happen to me. I know he wouldn't."

No, he wouldn't. Even if we didn't know what *this* was, we knew Hector wouldn't let it happen to either of us.

It really was the only option that made any sense. Either Hector was home free by now, or he was in this room taking the cat-o'-nine-tails to cure him of his urge to get physical. If they were in there . . . I wouldn't want to be us.

"Well," I said, "if you're gonna do it, do it."

As I said it, Skitz snapped the doorknob and threw the door open with the kind of come-and-get-it bravado that would have scared the Untouchables.

The door swung and bounced off the wall as we bounded into the room.

The lights were on. It was warm. It was empty.

Empty, of course, except for the life-size oil paintings of Jesus and Mary and a couple of popes that dominated three of the high wood-paneled walls in the eighteen-foot cube of a room. Along one wall was a bank of closet doors holding the rainbow of vestments the priests got into for services, and directly across from us were three big red leather throne chairs sitting under a rocket of a stained-glass window depicting St. Francis of Assisi and all his animal pals.

So it almost didn't feel like we were alone. But thank God we were.

The two of us were lightly panting as we walked across and spilled ourselves into two of the chairs. We didn't like to admit it, but Father Shenanigan intimidated the bejeesus out of us.

"See," I said between tom-tom heartbeats, "I told you they were gone."

Skitz already had his breath back. And his mania. "Ya, maybe," he said. He hopped right up again from the throne, and marched back out of the sacristy.

"Right," I said, "back to work." I knew he wasn't going back to work.

When we were out the door he turned right instead of the appropriate left.

"C'mon, Skitz," I said.

"I just want to take one walk around," he said. "C'mon, Drew, you love walking around when nobody's here."

"No," I said adamantly, "we have to work or we're gonna catch it."

"Suit yourself," he said.

I stood watching him head down the aisle. "Aw, hell," I said, and chased again.

We strode down the long side aisle, past rows and rows of shiny oak pews on our left, past the confessionals on our right, then the high bank of devotional candles where you're supposed to leave a donation and light a candle, and half of them were unlit. We walked under one after another stained-glass window, under one after another amazing giant ceiling painting of one more Gospel scene. The angles and the domes and the tapestries and the stonework were as much like a Russian palace as a church, and after all my time there I could not walk through the place without staring all around like a tourist, or without shivering.

But there was no sign of human folk, and that was good.

At the very back of the church was a massive balcony with wildly creaky stairs at either side curling up to an area for a choir and a glorious monster of a pipe organ that was built right into the church when it was put together 150 years ago, and which had such a sound God could not ignore it wherever He was, whatever He was doing. The balcony was made so you could never see who was up there unless you were up there, making it all the more eerie, godlike, and humbling.

When we had made it all the way the length of the church Skitz did not even hesitate to mount the stairs.

Each stair creaked like a snapping tree limb.

He got as far as three.

"Get back to work," Father Shenanigan's voice boomed, from high above us and about thirty feet below the ground.

I nearly choked. I started backpedaling, walking back up the aisle. I waited for Skitz to come back down. He stood still.

"We were looking for Hector," Skitz said.

"Hector is gone. I told you to get back to work."

Skitz still waited. You would have to know Skitz to know this, but I could see just from the way he was, from the hunch of his back and his grip on the rail, that he was thinking about it. He was thinking about risking it all and defying Father and going right up those stairs.

He decided just to risk some of it.

"We're finished working," Skitz lied.

Holy smokes.

The emptiness of the giant of a church was so complete just then. The silence was so total I felt sure if I strained any harder to hear something I would hear confessions from ten years ago.

Father broke it, though.

"Then go," he growled, and it rolled out, down from the balcony, up the center aisle, off the altar, and all the way back down again. And it rolled and it rolled until it chased us right out the back door of the church.

JESUS, MARY, AND ST. JOSEPH ASPIRIN

"DREW, DREW, YOU GOTTA COME OUT."

I was really going to have to brick up that window.

"Come on. I got St. Joes and RC Colas."

It was Hector. I didn't answer him, and he didn't need me to because he knew I was going to come, and he knew I was going to come because that was the drill, and not because he had St. Joes and RCs.

St. Joseph aspirin, which tasted kind of like Tang in pill form, and Royal Crown Cola. To us, our little cult, these were the things. These were our Communion, our wafers and wine, our body and blood. These were the items that brought Skitz, Hector, and me together around a table.

Even if around a table actually meant around a tree. And even if it was around four o'clock in the morning.

Especially if it was around four o'clock in the morning.

There was nobody outside my window by the time I got outside, but I wasn't dreaming. I dream a lot better than that, so I knew it was real, they were real, and they were going to meet me. I made my way down the street, down the hill, across the parkway, across the field, alongside the Muddy River, until I reached our tree, which everybody knows as the Pulpit Elm.

It was everybody's tree, I suppose. You could hardly expect to keep a tree like the Pulpit Elm to yourself. It was one of a kind, a fat sprawling mutant of two great elm trees spliced together but still trying to pull apart. And in the middle there, in the split that never quite split, somebody sometime had the wild idea to build this stairway-to-heaven deal. Using flat stones and slate, they built a full set of steps that lead you right up and *into* the tree until you get about eighteen feet high, and there it all ends with a kind of a seat and almost a podium. When you get there, you are hanging right out over the slow sloppy Muddy, so that if it ever really was used as a pulpit, it was for preaching to frogs and fishes.

No one ever had any information as to how the tree got that way, it was just there forever and would continue to be there forever. And though I know forever doesn't really exist, I also know we are talking about the life span of an elm tree, which is about as forever as a person could ever need.

I walked up the uneven stairs to find Hector sitting on the seat at the top, and Skitz a few steps down from him. What little light there was was provided by one pale moon and a string of streetlights lining the parkway fifty yards up field.

I stared up. They stared down. They looked a little ghostly. Hector stood ominously, looking down with his trusty hockey stick like a staff in his hand, like Moses or the Grim Reaper.

"Did somebody mention St. Joes and RCs?" I asked.

I didn't see Hector's little flick of a tossing motion, and the bottle of St. Joseph aspirin bopped me right in the mouth. "Ow."

"Good thing you have some aspirin," Skitz said, stepping down to hand me a Royal Crown Cola.

First thing I did was pour a good mouthful of St. Joes in my mouth and chew them up. It was always a fresh joy, tasting the sour-sweet orange surge that clung to my tongue and throat. Then I popped open the RC and chased the aspirin right down into my belly. When the mix took hold of me, I felt like a human bottle rocket.

"Thanks," I said, throwing the bottle back to Hector. He had no trouble catching it.

Skitz was popping pills in his mouth and chewing away like a zoo monkey, guzzling cola, then doing it all again.

"So," I said, "who's got company tonight?"

Skitz raised his hand. "I was lying in my bed, listening. I heard them coming, couldn't believe it, as the footsteps came closer and closer like a friggin' slasher movie. Then they came in my room, while I was rolled over, faking like mad, trying to be asleep. They hovered there over me for about a thousand minutes before he blessed me. He *blessed* me, right there in my own bed. I'll tell ya, I had my fist jammed right up in my mouth to keep from screaming. I couldn't wait to get my ass out of that bed, and as soon as my door was shut again

I was up and out that window like a damn squirrel."

Whatever St. Joes were left in his hand, Skitz stuffed them all and chewed away.

"Drew, man, my bed is *blessed* now and everything. What am I gonna do?"

"Can't do what you were doing before, that's for sure."

"Wouldja shuddup with that? I wasn't even doing anything, there was no need to come and bless me. Jeez."

I realized then that Hector was being totally silent, and wasn't even looking down my way anymore. He had gotten up and swung around to the lectern part of the pulpit, and was having more to do with the frogs and the fishes than the Drews and the Skitzes. I gestured, double-jerking my thumb toward Hector for a what's-up from Skitz.

"Don't ask me," Skitz said. "He's Mister Weird, Hector the Spectre, can't get anywhere near him."

"How'd you get him out, then?" I asked. When he was Hector the Spectre, no way could Skitz pull him outside without me.

"I didn't. He was already out. I found him on your

lawn when I got there. Just staring like a freak."

Oh my. How many nut trees can spring up in my garden in the middle of the night before people begin to notice? How long was he out there?

I brushed past Skitz, who was heading downstairs anyway. "I'm going for a walk," he said.

There was a little humming noise coming off Hector as I came up behind him in the pulpit. He was leaning hard over the lectern, hovering over the water. I could hear the motion of the Muddy below us, but just barely. The Muddy hardly moved.

"How's it?" I asked from behind him.

The little humming noise continued.

I tried again. "How's it, Hector?"

The humming stopped.

There was a slight increase in the water noise coming from below. It was actually kind of splashy.

"I almost caught a frog," Skitz called up.

"That's good, Skitz," I said. "Are you in the water, numbnuts? If you are in the water, man you are going to freeze to death. Your pants and shoes and socks are going to be soaked, and you are going to freeze. It is freezing, Skitz." It wasn't freezing. In fact, for the time of year it was pretty warm. But when dealing with Skitz you could never risk understating a thing. And unseasonably warm or no, if you got wet, it would be wicked.

There was an increase of rustling, splashy noise from down there, then a pause.

"No. I am not in the water."

I was standing right behind Hector, who was leaning out over the water. "Is he out of the water, Hec?"

He did the little hum again, followed by, "We have no violence here."

I waited. "O-kay," I said. "I didn't ask you to shoot him, I just asked if he was out of the water."

Hector turned around to face me. "We have no violence here, Drew," he said in a spook voice that didn't belong to him or to anybody else I knew. "That's what they keep saying to me."

"Who's they?"

"I caught a frog," Skitz called from a ways away.

"Good, eat it and shuddup," I called.

"The Fathers, they all keep telling me, we have no violence here."

"Which Fathers, Hector?"

"All of them. The Fathers from Blessed Sacrament. And my mother. They been talking. They've been talking, like I got a problem and it needs to be dealt with."

"You don't got any problem. That's stupid. Everybody hits Skitz. That's no kind of violence. Even Skitz doesn't care. Hey, Skitz," I called.

"Ya?"

"How long did it take you to forget about it after Hector kicked you around yesterday?"

There was silence. Sometimes, you have to give Skitz something like commercial breaks, talk about one thing when he's thinking about another one.

"Did you eat that frog, Skitz?"

"Shuddup, I never ate no frog, and Hector didn't kick me around yesterday."

"Yes, he did."

"Ah, no, he didn't."

"Ah, yes, I did."

"Ah, no, you didn't."

"Sheesh, you are so frustrating. I want to come down and kick you around right now."

"Well, come on down, big boy."

Hector stomped the first step down the Pulpit Elm

steps, but I stopped him. "I think we proved the point already. Your conscience should be clear."

"Well, it's not. They keep saying there's something wrong with me and we gotta work on it, and my family, they take this stuff seriously, man. They take whatever the priests and the nuns say as coming straight from Jesus, Mary, and Joseph themselves." Angry as he was, he still bowed his head at Jesus. "Now I'm supposed to be under Father's *wing*. Drew, man, he's taking me under his *wing*."

"I think he wants to take you under his drumstick, myself," Skitz called.

Ooooh, man. Why, Skitz, why, oh why?

Hector went rigid with rage, and suddenly everything seemed easier to see as white light appeared to emit out of his eyes and bathe all our surroundings. He made a grunt and gestured with his thumb in the general direction of Skitz Fitzsimmons's foolish and suicidal voice.

"Ya, go on," I said, waving Hector past me like a cop waving a speeding car past an accident. Or toward one.

"Oh!" Skitz screamed as the reality and the fists hit him. "Oh, jeez . . . no . . ." It went on that way for about a minute, the sounds getting progressively Batman—"*Ooof . . . bwooor . . . huunnn . . .*"—until it all came to a sudden end with a big splash.

Hector came back around the tree and met me at the bottom of the stairs. We both sat down on the ground cross-legged, facing each other, and pulled two more RCs off the plastic ring. I pulled the tab off my can and put it on my pinky like a ring. He tapped out a few St. Joes into my palm and I ate them. He ate a fistful and we listened to the splashing and splucking of Skitz working his way back up the bank of the Muddy.

"We have no violence here," I said.

Hector was unamused. "We have no violence here," he said flatly, as if he was saying entirely different words from mine.

"Tell me something. When Shenanigan pulled you away from us yesterday, did we have violence here?"

Hector sat there, and stared. Then he sat there, and he stared. The nutty humming came back to him, and he stared. And he hummed.

"I'll take that as a yes, then?" I asked.

He hummed, which didn't help me entirely, since the hum probably meant whatever it meant the first time.

"I think Father Shenanigan is a creep," I said, since it was true, whatever else was true.

"Maybe it's me, it's my fault," Hector croaked. "Maybe I ask for it. Maybe I want it."

I got a shiver. A real one, like a cold wind slicing through me though there was no wind, and my shoulders shook visibly. It was the feeling I get when I see a rat, and there were plenty of water rats along the Muddy—fat, foul, rotten rats. I shivered again.

"It's not your fault. Anyway, *what's* your fault? Anyway, shuddup. Whenever they act like power-freak jerks and go overboard they try to make you feel like it's your fault, but don't let them. You're practically perfect, man. You are like the kid they would build in their laboratory if they could, and then they would clone you and bump off the rest of us."

He looked up at me, a complete blank. His face looked puffy and old and tired, but that could have been the light.

In a second, though, that changed.

His eyes flashed, his face creased with bolts of intensity, he grabbed his hockey stick and lunged right past me.

I threw myself sideways to avoid him, then looked back to see him laying into a spitting slob of a giant rat with a bald fleshy eighteen-inch tail.

"Jesus," I said, squirming along the ground, away. Hector was on him, though, on him like a murderer, hacking, pounding, chopping, chopping, chopping the rat so hard with his stick you could catch the sight of blood balls that looked like wet Milk Duds shooting every which way, catching the moonlight.

Hector grunted hard with every chop and added a little sad moan as he poured himself into the job of killing that rat four times beyond being well and truly dead.

"Hector," I said calmly, getting to my feet and approaching him. He kept hitting it. "Hector, come on. You did it. Come on." Nobody wanted to see a rat dead more than I did, but I didn't want to see this.

I think he just ran out of steam eventually. He got slower and slower and then his motion stopped. He was still on his knees. I didn't want to go nearer, but I did. I took his arm and pulled him up. You could hardly tell there was ever an animal there, as opposed to, say, a watermelon. I took his stick away from him, and he just let go. I tugged him away until we were halfway down to where Skitz was, at the water.

"Numbnuts, we're going," I called down to the water.

When Skitz finally made his way back up, looking more than a little *Creature from the Black Lagoon*, Hector hopped to attention, and came over all motherly. He pulled off his heavy wool navy peacoat and draped it over Skitz. He also gave him the bottle of St. Joseph aspirin out of the pocket, which Skitz finished in a gulp, and popped open the last Royal Crown Cola for him.

It could be one million degrees below zero and we would always think cola was the right idea.

"We have no violence here," Hector said sadly, grabbing Skitz around the shoulders and pulling him rough close.

"Except sometimes," Skitz said brightly.

Hector hauled him in harder.

It was starting to get light. We could get Skitz back now and see if it was clear to go home. It would be, because like vampires, the nighttime callers couldn't bear the unforgiving light of day.

CHRISTIAN SCIENCE

OUR FAVORITE SPECTATOR SPORTS WERE WRESTLING, hockey, and standing around the John Hancock Tower waiting to see the next windowpane pop out. It had a history, the Hancock, starting from before it was even completed. The great big windows would jump out when the wind blew, which was a fairly serious thing, and eventually every last one had to be redone. Still, every now and then one would come loose for old time's sake and they'd rope off that side of the building for a few days in case it became a trend again.

I couldn't resist this. Whenever it showed up in my stack of morning *Globe*s, I made a point to get down there and watch, like some folks watch planes, waiting to see where the glass would land, and if it would slice right through somebody. The damage would be horrific, since each huge mirror window was six feet by eight feet and must have weighed half a ton, and some of them were up there a zillion feet off the ground, since this was now famously the tallest building in all New England. Even if it was still spitting out its teeth all over the place.

But it was a thrill, I have to confess, an honest-to-God morbid thrill, hanging out there, waiting for something almighty awful to happen to some poor chump. I went on my own more often than not, not because this was what I would call an actual *guilty* pleasure—I wasn't having any of that baloney—but because Hector believed it was some kind of sin to be praying for decapitations, and Skitz just frankly could not be trusted around the John Hancock Tower work site.

Because of all the trouble they'd had with the glass, they were forced to put up a big barrier on the ground floor of the window-popper side so you couldn't get right up close to the building. I personally didn't think that made a whole lot of difference, because if one of those sheets jumped out of its frame and caught that wicked swirling Copley Square wind it was as likely to land in Revere as it was to fall straight down to the street below. But they were the construction experts and they had their figures on where the things would fall, and so who was I to disagree, even if they also had their figures on how to fit glass into New England's highest office tower, and look where that got them.

Anyway, they were serious about it, and nobody was allowed inside the getting-killed-by-the-glass barrier.

So, you could not keep Skitz outside the getting-killed-by-the-glass barrier. Anytime we got near the place he was like a demented metal ball bearing, pulled by the steel frame of the Hancock, under the barrier and right up flat to the building. He walked along it, touching it lightly with his hands, looking straight up into the sky. Ever do that? Ever look along a big building straight up into the sky, especially a huge glass tower? Disorienting. You can't do it without getting the sensation of everything moving, the sidewalk under you and the monstrosity in front of you, as the clouds sail past the edge of the structure way, way up there. And it doesn't help any that the Hancock actually *does* wobble. Skitz would get that sensation, and he'd love

"You come here often?" Father Mullarkey's big bear voice said from right next to me.

I wasn't startled exactly, because before I heard him, I saw him there, the hazy, reflected him in the Hancock glass. Maybe I was startled anyway, a little.

"Ya," I said, because unless I have a good reason not to, I always answer directly and honestly.

"Waiting to see somebody cut up, are you?"

That question could constitute a good reason. I stopped looking at blue me and him and went to looking up, and up.

"'Course not, Father, that would be a sin."

"Only if you were actually doing the cutting."

"Oh. Oh, well, that's good to know. Why are you here?"

"Waiting to see somebody get cut up," Father said.

"Really?"

"Sure. It's a rush. I've been making this pilgrimage for a long time, since this was still a building site. Should have seen it in those days, boy, mirrors flying through the sky every which way so you didn't know where to run, cops chasing everybody away. . . . Between the adrenaline and the dizziness of looking up at the flying mirrors in the sky, I don't think I've quite matched that thrill to this day. I keep watching for a decapitation, though, that'd probably top it."

"Wow. And you're allowed?"

"Absolutely. It's death, baby. Catholic sport writ large. We're practically *required* to be morbid. In fact, if I remember, I think I had to take a vow of morbidity, along with the other ones . . . most of which I can't remember."

Ordinary circumstances would have me cursing my luck, running into a priest in the real world. Father Mullarkey had a knack for suspending regular circumstances.

"Cool," I said, scanning ever harder for panes of glass that were iffy. "Then that's really what I was here for too."

"What?" Father boomed, making me jump now and look at the in-the-flesh him. "Then you lied. And that *is* a sin. That is a direct violation of one of the Seven Commandments."

"There are ten."

"Three of them are questionable, so I don't enforce. Would you like to go over to Newbury Comics?

Nobody's going to die here today. Weather's too nice."

"Which Commandments don't you enforce?"

"Depends on your reference. You talking Deuteronomy, or Exodus?"

"What?"

"Right. Let's go to Newbury Comics."

Newbury Comics was a record store. I had been in it exactly never, because music doesn't interest me much, and stores interest me even less.

"Why would we want to go there?" I asked.

He looked at me as if I'd asked him if Jesus was a Communist.

"Because there is music in there," he said finally, grinning at me like a mad genius.

I waited. That was it, apparently.

"So, why do you want me to go?"

"Because, my son," Father said, resting a big paw on my shoulder and turning me up Boylston Street away from the Hancock, "I am a messenger of The Lord. And The Lord tells me that you do not get The Message."

Jeez, what does a guy say to that? What does a guy say to that, to a priest?

"Would it be one of the Seven Deadly Sins to say that I think The Lord is mistaken?"

"There are only five. The other two are utter nonsense."

"So—"

"No. But it would be blaspheming."

"What is blaspheming, exactly, anyway?"

"Blaspheming . . . would be like saying Led Zeppelin is better than the Rolling Stones. Understand?"

"No."

"My God, boy, we've got to get you to Newbury Comics."

So we walked through Copley Square, then up Boylston, up almost to New England's formerly tallest structure, the Prudential Building. We crossed the street, zigged over to Newbury, and zagged up toward Mass. Ave. There we entered Newbury Comics. Everybody talked about Newbury Comics like it was just the hippest thing happening. Goin' to Newbury Comics, goin' to Newbury Comics. It was like an actual *thing*, to do. Thousands of times, I'd hear guys say, Goin' to Newbury Comics on Saturday, then they'd be off downtown, be gone pretty much the whole day, then come back with nothing. Whatcha do today? Went to Newbury Comics. Get anything? Nah. How was it? It was *un-believable*, man.

And that was the part I could believe, that it was unbelievable. What *was* the thing with music? I never got it. It was just a record store.

"Can you believe it?" Father said as we stepped up the stairs, through the doors, into Newbury Comics and into some squall of noises from speakers aimed right at us like those pictures whose eyes seem to follow you around the room.

"I don't know what it is, Father, so I don't know if I can believe it or not."

"It's Ten Years After, my son, and you'd better believe it."

Father spooked me just a little bit at that point, standing still in a very prominent spot a few feet inside the door, closing his eyes, and having some kind of religious-type moment with the music. He winced, smiled, gritted his teeth, wagged his head rhythmically from side to side, and appeared to join the singer in lipping the words, even though he could have been speaking in tongues for all the sense it made to me. And the song went on for about an hour.

"Don't you get embarrassed, even a little?" I asked as the noodly guitar finally started trailing off.

"Certainly not," he said, his eyes still closed. "It's rock 'n' roll, man."

"Oh," I said.

He nodded, like that settled that. Then he tugged me by the arm, downstairs into the world of vinyl record albums, posters, T-shirts, and all things rocking.

Which, I may have mentioned, was a world that held little allure for me.

I just didn't get it, music. I didn't *hear* it, in the way that other people heard music. It was like a very foreign language, or monkey chatter, or most of the Bible to me. I was aware of the sounds, but they did not move me in any way.

So it was kind of sad, the way Father Mullarkey raced from one bin to another, getting excited as a giant bearded baby as he scooped up one freako-looking psychedelic album after another by bands called Santana, The Grateful Dead, Jefferson Airplane, Cream, Love, and Big Brother and the Holding Company, and tucking them under his arm greedily just in case some similar freak came along and wanted what Father wanted. He really loved this stuff, and he was doing his best to explain that love to me, and I was doing my best to be polite about it. I even managed to stay right with him for a while. But when I caught him drifting as he buried his face in the whole catalogue of Creedence Clearwater Revival, I slipped away and leaned on the nearest hard surface.

"Can I help you?" the skinny, flat-voiced Newbury Comics clerk said.

He had his bright red Newbury Comics shirt on, with the name of the store on it, NEWBURY COMICS, and the name of himself on it, DARYL, but all the same I didn't feel like respecting his authority. He weighed less than me.

Accordingly, I just stared at him.

"Are you buying something, or are you just looking for someplace to hang out?"

"Of course he's buying," Father said, sidling up next to me, clutching what had to be a good two dozen albums. Then he reached into the stack and drew out a copy of *The Best of Ten Years After*. "God told me to get you this, Andrew," he said proudly. "It will help you see the light. You'll see."

"Right," Daryl said, looking at Father the same suspicious way he looked at me. "I'll, ah, just take you at this register here."

"Groovy," Father said, miraculously making things even more mortifying than they already were.

When Father Mullarkey had finally completed his purchase of every record in the shop that looked as if the cover had been painted by a demented four-year-old, we beat it back out to Newbury Street, to Boylston Street, across the Prudential Center, on through the big sprawl of the new Christian Science Center. It was one of the nicest places in town to walk through, I thought, lots of wide spaces, a modern building with odd angles, crisp angles all orderly, corridors and flat columns like upturned louvre slats. Churchy but not, all of it open and airy and built around this reflecting pool that was the size of a football field and gave you the impression that you were looking across to the water tipping off the edge of the world.

"Don't get me wrong," Father blurted, yanking me off of reflecting over the reflecting pool. "I have a lot of appreciation for these guys." He gestured with his thumb toward the Christian Science Reading Room. "Nice reading rooms, nice newspaper, nice architecture, and you have to love a religion founded by a lady. But how can you expect to run a faith with neither alcohol *nor* medications? Is that any way to operate a proper opiate of the people? It can't be done."

I didn't even get a chance to register how lost and alarmed I was by the conversation before Father erupted into fits of huge haw laughs that skimmed across the surface of the Christian Science water and echoed around the whole of downtown Boston. So I laughed some, to do my bit, until he petered out.

We continued on out, through the grubbed-up little maze of streets, down St. Stephen running behind Symphony Hall, and out to Huntington Avenue by Northeastern University. There we waited for the trolley.

He was funny now in a different way. Not humorous, but funny. He suddenly lost the big-swagger, big-voice stuff, and stared way far off into space. It was like he had just heard some bad news, though nobody had said a thing. He clutched his Newbury Comics bag full of records to his chest like you'd hold a baby or a puppy or all your belongings if you lived in the street.

We waited ten minutes for the tin can of a streetcar to come clanging up out of the ground and stop in front of us with a squeal. We still said nothing as we made our way to the back of the near-empty car. Father sat down first, in the backmost double bench seat. I took the one directly in front of him, and stretched my leg across it and my arm across the seat-back. The way you do when you're talking to your pal on the trolley.

"Are you all right?" I asked him.

"I am incredibly hungry," he said.

The trolley hurtled—as much as they can hurtle—up Huntington Avenue, shaking violently side to side like the tail of a gigantic metal dog, bouncing us off the hard molded fiberglass seats.

He reached into the bag, drew out my album, and handed it over.

"You didn't really need to do that, Father," I said.

Some of his energy came back and he smiled broadly. "It was only right. I do feel a responsibility to bring you The Word. And, God told me to."

I couldn't have been less interested in The Word. He must have known that. Did he know that? Should I tell him? That would be impolite. I'm a lot of things, but not that. Anyway, he must know. How much does he know?

A lot, I figured.

"Can I ask you something, Father?"

"You can ask me a million somethings if you want to. I might even answer some." He stared out the window, his forehead bouncing like a handball off the glass.

"How come you guys are all so hard on Hector?"

"Because he needs it."

"I don't think anybody needs that."

"He's wayward."

"Wayward? I don't know which *way* you're referring to, but Hector Fossas is about the most Dudley Do-Right guy there is."

"He is decent, of course he is. But he has his problems as well. Monsignor has filled me in on all the histories in our parish. He is a good boy, a strong boy, but that strength cuts both ways, can even be dangerous. He's an angry guy, our Hector. He needs guidance. He needs proper male influence. Good, Christian male guidance."

"That's his dad. His dad is good, Christian male guidance."

"Which would be fine if his dad were there."

He was still relatively new on the scene, since he hadn't been here for generations like most of us and our families. That's why he was still an outsider. That's why he couldn't know everything, and I'd have to allow for that and be patient with him and maybe even help him out a bit. Take him under my wing, even.

"His dad is there, Father."

"No, he isn't. He hasn't been there for months now."

"No offense, Father Mullarkey, but I don't think you know what you're talking about. I would know something like that, if it was true, so it can't be true."

He stopped looking out the window and looked intensely at me. "No offense to you either, Drew. I appreciate what you're saying, but it is true. We have spent quite a bit of time with Hector's family over the months, his mother has asked for our support, and I'm afraid this is very much true. But we are helping them. They are a family of great strength and faith, and so they will be all right. Just have trust, have faith. Come on, let's eat."

It was not my stop, but Father tugged me by the sleeve and we got off in front of Papa Gino's Pizza.

"I don't have any money," I said as he towed me inside.

"I'm buying," he said.

"I'll be having my dinner at home in just a couple of hours."

"You're a growing boy, you'll be hungry again by then."

This was true, but still I couldn't help feeling a little wrong about it all.

Double cheese, pepperoni, and sausage helped me feel a little righter about it, however. Papa Gino's was like a drug to me. Just the suggestion of it could make me do anything.

Father ate most of it, though, and most of the basket of fries that he ordered with it. We both sucked on large Cokes, sitting in the back room with the yellowed mirrors and the cracked Formica booths.

"You're really not lying, right? About Hector's father and all."

His mouth was full. He shook his head.

"Why would he never tell me? Why would he pretend all this time that his father was still there?"

He swallowed. "His family considers the situation a tremendous shame. They are intensely proud folks. They are feeling a lot of humiliation, and guilt."

"Guilt?" I said, gnawing on my crust and trying hard not to snatch the last slice of pizza. "Guilt? Why should they feel guilty? Why should Hector, or his mother, or whoever else is still there in the house and who did not run out on anybody, why should *they* feel guilty?"

Father eyed the lone pizza slice. He wanted it as badly as I did, I knew. We both let it sit there on the table between us.

"Guilt," he said slowly, "is a funny, funny thing."

"Ya," I said, "it makes me laugh all the time."

"It is a powerful force, guilt. People can impose it on themselves with very little provocation, and it can weigh on them so heavily they can be crushed by it. Some truly innocent people can be overcome with guilt, and then again, there are other people who are all but incapable of feeling any guilt at all, even when they should."

"That would be Skitz," I said. "But it's not just guilt, there are lots of things he can't feel, like fear and heat and cold."

"Yes, Skitz Fitzsimmons," Father said in a really loaded, doubtful voice. Then he picked up the remaining slice, tore it in half like you would with a sheet of paper, and handed me mine.

I felt suddenly really awful for Hector, for the basic fact that his father left him, and even more for the fact that he had to feel so humiliated about it that he had to hide. That wasn't right. I mean, his people were good people, they were famous almost, as genuine and religious and devout Catholics and all that, but I couldn't shake the feeling that it was nasty, a goodness that made them feel so bad about something that wasn't even their fault.

But I also found myself feeling that this guy here with the records, this guy tearing his last slice in half to feed the rabble, was not a bad choice for Hector to have helping him out. I could feel okay about that.

"Is it true Hector wants to become a priest when he's older?"

I nodded. "He made up his mind when he was six, and hasn't changed it. When my dog Freckles got hit by a car, he gave her the Last Rites. Then he said a whole service over her when we buried her, put down a funeral wreath that he bought with his own money and everything. And he gave me grief counseling for about two weeks."

Father smiled broadly and shook his shaggy head. "We certainly could use more men like him," he said.

I stood when I had finished my last bite and Father was picking at the remaining fries. He had them drenched in ketchup and mustard, possibly as a defense against me asking for any more.

"I really should be going," I said, scooping up my album. I sort of waved it at him, thinking at the same time I didn't even have anything to play it on. Why would he even think I had an old vinyl-record player? "Thank you, for this," I said then, waving the album at the food, "and for that."

He nodded, folded his hands. "I like to meet the people of the parish. I like to be out and about. It can be a lonely life sometimes, this. Especially when they move you around every couple of years, you don't really get to know people that well."

"Why do they move you, then?"

Father shrugged. "It's just what they do. Ours is not to question why . . ."

I thought about it, because it sounded like one of those things you were supposed to think about.

"Why is it not?" I asked.

He laughed. "You sure you have to be going? I'd like to let you hear some of these records. And we could play your record. . . . You'd be very impressed, I think."

If, on the spectrum of irresistible offers, Papa Gino's was sitting at one end, then hanging out listening to that stack of records was at the other.

"Sorry, really do have to go, Father. Maybe another time."

"Okay, then," he said as I backed off from the booth. "We will do it another time." He quickly buried himself again in his messy fries, his face becoming obscured as his hair hung down and met up with the basket. Like he was trying to hide in his food.

I had just hit the sidewalk when I caught the thought: Where was he supposed to play me those albums? Was I just invited to listen to records at his house?

His house was the rectory, after all.

NO VIOLENCE HERE

"HEY, HECTOR, WHERE IS YOUR FATHER?"

"Hey, shuddup, Drew, that's where he is. How am I supposed to know where he is right now? You know where your old man is right this minute?"

He was sitting a little behind me, a little off my left shoulder. There was the shadow of him in the corner of my eye so his presence was very there, but it wasn't so heavy as it would have been if I was looking right at him. So I could talk.

"Ya. Unless he got hit by a car crossing the street, he's leaning over the bar at Doyle's right now."

"Good, fine, why don't you just go meet him, then?"

"Why didn't you tell me, Hector? You knew you

could tell me anything. Why didn't you tell me your old man left?"

"My old man didn't leave, that's why."

"Yes, he did."

We were down at the Muddy River, the far side this time, the nicer side. It was sunny daylight, and we were sitting on the grassy flat bit we called the peninsula that stuck right out and made the water go around us. Whenever there was sun it seemed to settle here on the Brookline side because of all the trees crowding our side. Trees are fine too, of course, but it just made you feel like Brookline was the place of light and we were the place of dark, and Brookline always got all the good stuff.

We were looking back out over in the direction of home. Ducks swam up to us and away again when they caught on we weren't handing out food today. We were surrounded by little and not-so-little mines of goose turds that still didn't make the place any less nice to sit, as long as you watched yourself.

"No, he didn't," Hector said in his warning voice, which is about two degrees warmer than his threatening voice.

"Then how come you told the Fathers that he did?"

He didn't answer right away, which was a little chilling, as this was a tense conversation and Hector could be a shade edgy. But it was okay just the same because this was still Hector, and this was still me.

Thump. I felt the whole of Hector hit my back and the whole of both of us hit the ground. The air blasted right out of my lungs, making me cough up a sound like a sea lion. My arms were stretched out ahead of me in a Superman flying position, and I was pinned solid to the ground just like that. My temple was pressed well into a lump of goose dump.

Hector leaned right down over my other ear. His scapular, which he always wore—the cloth postage-stamp-on-a-string with the picture of Jesus—spilled out of his shirt and lay there on my cheek.

"I didn't tell any Fathers anything," he said in a cracked voice that would make you wonder which of us was pinned to the ground. "And you're not gonna tell anybody anything either. Why would I say something so embarrassing about my own family, huh? Why would I do something that stupid?"

The only embarrassment and stupidity I could see

here was me, trying to speak with half a mouth and a head planted in goose crap.

"There's no humiliation in it, you know, Hector."

"Shuddup. What would you know? How would you like it if it happened to you, Drew?"

I wasn't at all sure how I would feel about that. I attempted to shrug. Felt pretty stupid in the attempt.

"Can I get up, Hector? Would you let me up now, please?"

That was what you could expect of Hector. The kind of guy who would get you down, but the kind of guy who would let you up, and dust you off.

He didn't let me up.

This, I had to say, made me nervous.

"Hec?" I said.

He leaned more heavily into me, lay right down on top of me.

"I'm sorry," he whispered, not to upset the ducks.

" 'Sokay," I said.

"We have no violence here," he said.

"I know we don't," I said.

Hector rolled off me then, just flop-rolled like a dummy. He lay on his back, looking at the sky while I got myself off the ground and slapped all the nasty off of me.

"We been together a long time, huh," he said.

"Ya, we have."

"You know, Drew, you know all the times when you would fall behind, and I would always wait up for you?"

"I do know that. Of course I know that. How could I ever not know that?"

"Well, if I'm ever, y'know, falling behind, will you wait for me? Will you wait up for me? Will you don't let me fall too far behind?"

I stared down at him. I didn't like what I saw. I turned my back on him so I could look at the trees on our side of the river.

"That's a stupid question," I said.

"Well, I'm a stupid guy," he said rapidly. "And I need an answer out loud."

"I'll wait for ya, stupid. I wouldn't ever let you fall behind. I'll always wait up." I waited, then I shouted. "Okay! Is that out-loud enough for you?"

"Ya," he said, still lying still, "just about."

BELIEVE

"DON'T TOY WITH ME."

"I'm not kidding."

"Then you're lying."

"I don't lie."

"Meathead, you know Hector doesn't lie."

"Of course he does. Everybody lies. No offense, Hec."

"None taken," he said calmly. Then he punched him, calmly, right in that spot on the side of the head where it feels like there's no bone protecting your brain.

"Ow. Now you gotta give me some St. Joes."

"I don't have any. But I can give you some St. *Shuddup.*"

"Hector, please. The tickets."

"I got them at home. Three tickets, this Saturday night, Boston Garden. He just gave them to me, just like he said."

"Just like that?" Skitz asked.

"Just like that."

He was referring to the Bruins tickets that were announced as part of the package when Hector was awarded the coveted Altar Boy of the Year prize. It came with, in descending order of desirability, the hockey tickets, a trophy as tall as the Stanley Cup, and an endless crapstorm of jokes about what a guy had to do to win Altar Boy of the Year.

"You have them, or you *have* them? You have them in your actual possession, as in you have seen them and touched them and they are safe, rather than you have heard about them or been promised them or—"

"Jeez, you don't believe nothin' do you, Drew?"

"No, I don't. I don't believe in believing."

By the time Saturday came around, I was ready to repent and believe. Just this once. The tickets were for real, and there were no strings attached except for the obvious big string of having to be an altar boy to win them, and then having to be the Altar Boy of Altar Boys to boot.

I was not an altar boy. I had never been one and never would be one even though my two closest associates always were. And even though at times the recruitment pressure to bring me into the team could be Mafia-level persuasive.

And what did they care, anyway? Were there skills, talents, traits that marked you out as a grade-A altar boy prospect? If there were, I was certain not to have them, but Monsignor Blarney and Father Shenanigan were forever at me to join the team, and once Father Mullarkey came along and threw his weight into it, it took all my powers of apathy and evasion to hold them off.

So it was coming pretty close to the lions' den when I agreed to go on the Altar Boy of the Year trip to the Bruins game. Especially as the official escort was big ol' Mullarkey himself.

We met him at the trolley stop closest to the rectory. It was close enough that he could see us approach from his window, so he timed it just right for meeting the trolley and the three of us simultaneously. We jumped on, and Father insisted on taking care of the fares as the three of us headed for the back.

He hadn't even sat down before he got into it. "So, Andrew, when will you be joining your pals here and becoming an altar boy?"

Cripes.

"Well, Father, the team seems to be doing pretty well without me."

"We could always use more good men. I could see you winning the big prize yourself someday, just like Hector here."

"Hector here" frankly looked a little embarrassed at the mention.

"What about me, Father?" Skitz said. "I could win it."

He peered long at Skitz, puzzling him out, seeing if he was serious. "Sure," he answered, "I don't see why not."

He was being polite, of course, since everybody could see why not. But just for the record Skitz helped clarify. "And Drew, you get to tap into the wine they keep backstage," he blurted.

"Maybe I do see why not," Father added. But he laughed too, in a way the other priests probably wouldn't have, in a way more promising people than Skitz Fitzsimmons would not inspire.

"I'll give it some thought, Father," I said, the way I said it to him a couple of times before and the way I said it to the other ones lots and lots of times before. They had all the altar boys they needed. Even with Hector alone, they had all the altar boys they needed. Hell, he'd probably make a better priest than any of them, and run the whole school by himself.

And it was his night. Hector was the man of the evening, Father made sure everybody knew it, and we made sure we followed right along. We talked all the way in about Hector's greatness and worthiness for the historic award. Even if the greatness that got us to this point amounted to a collection of the most boring qualities Hector or anybody else could possess, we sang them up all the way downtown. Down South Huntington Avenue talking about Hector's amazing punctuality, never once being late even for the six-forty-five Mass on a Tuesday or a Wednesday morning in February when he and Father made up half the population of the service. Hector's unerring ability to ring the bells at precisely the second Father wanted them rung, and being sure to stifle them again before he spoke again. "I could never figure that one out," Skitz said, shaking his head in wonder. "I know," Father said, shaking his head the same. It could be a panic some days at Mass, when Skitz would ring the bells real loud in the middle of Father's sermon or the "I Believes" or something, and then he'd make it twice as bad by saying, "Sorry, Father, sorry Father," real loud right up there on the altar. Even the real churchies couldn't help laughing.

The trolley finally dipped underground at Northeastern as Father got all misty over Hector's serving at weddings and baptisms and funerals, especially funerals, when folks actually requested, *requested* that Hector be their altar boy, which happened often enough with priests but never, ever before with an altar boy. That was altar boy star power, right there.

We had promoted Hector to archbishop by the time we reached Arlington Street Station, and Deputy God by the time we were to switch trolleys at Park Street.

"I don't feel too good," said Hector, who had been

almost entirely silent till then. I figured he was just being modest, which would figure. He wasn't great with compliments, but I didn't realize it had gotten so bad that praise made him physically ill. "Could we just talk about the game for a while, huh?" he said finally, testily. "Remember, the Bruins? Hockey? Y'know?"

Of course we could talk about the Bruins. Normally no one had to ask me to talk about the Bruins. In fact, it was not unusual for people to ask me to stop talking about them.

"And can we walk?" he asked. "I'd really rather walk. Maybe I'll feel better."

Usually we would take one more short trip, one subway stop from Park Street to North Station. But it wasn't a bad walk either, even if it was December.

"Are you sure you're going to be all right?" Father asked as we headed up the stairs and out into the chill.

"I'll be okay. Just my stomach. Just a little jumpy."

"Maybe it's the excitement," Father said.

"I'm sure that's what it is," Hector said.

"I'm excited and my stomach doesn't hurt, ya big baby," Skitz added.

"Would you *like* it to hurt?" Hector said.

"See, Father, he's feeling better already," I said.

"We're talking about me again," Hector said. "I thought we were going to talk about the Bruins? I thought this was my night, and I thought we were going to talk about the Bruins?"

He was very serious about talking about the Bruins. Even by my standards, he was very serious about talking about the Bruins. He was also walking along with his hand flat on his stomach like he was holding back some eruption.

"Right," I said. "For starters, last year never happened. The Bruins did not lose last year in the first round to the New *stupid* York *stupid* Islanders. That was just a bad nightmare that never really happened. The Boston Bruins are this year's legitimate Stanley Cup contenders, because they are way overdue and because they are as good as any team out there this year, and for a lot of other very good reasons including—and correct me if I'm wrong here, Father—there *is* a God."

Father was in the spirit of the occasion. "I have it on good authority that there is, in fact, a God of some sort."

"See?" I said. "Always go to a Jesuit for the straight dope."

Father laughed. He laughed really hard. Harder than I thought the joke maybe earned, but it was welcome anyway and made Skitz laugh even harder and Hector smile, though he still held his stomach.

"And second, the Bruins will not lose tonight, not again, to the *Anaheim Mighty Ducks*. The Bruins will not, must not, dare not lose in Boston to the *Mighty Ducks* who, may I remind everybody, were created out of a Disney movie. Ducks are not mighty. They will not lose to such a team, because the Bruins won fifty-one games last year, even if last year did not happen, and the opposition have ducks on their shirts and play in California, where hockey is unnatural. And I know the Bruins lost to this team a month ago, but that was in *California*, and this is Earth.

"But mostly, the Bruins will not lose tonight because they would not do that to me. And they would not do that to the Altar Boy of the Year."

"That's right," shouted Skitz.

"You be quiet," I said, "because they *would* do it to you."

We were ready for this by the time we went through the turnstiles at the Garden, and walked the big broad ramps toward our seats in the balcony. When we found our section and walked out into the arena, the atmosphere was like a party. Everybody was happy, everybody was noisy. The lights were bright and the ice was so white it was like a giant oval sheet of polished platinum with the big beautiful Bruins *B* painted in the middle of it. You could not fight it no matter how hard you tried: if you were in the building, you were in the mood.

"Yeeee-hooo!" Skitz screamed, like we were at a rodeo, long before there was any action to scream for.

Father laughed out loud. Father was a sport, I had to say. He thought everything was fun, and funny. "I'm going to go get us some drinks," he said.

"Go with him, Skitz," I said.

"Why?" He deflated, like it was a punishment.

"To help him carry, dummy." I sat down next to Hector, who still wasn't looking so hot. "Go on, will ya?"

When they were gone, I turned to Hector. "What's up? You gonna be all right?"

He nodded. The Zamboni machine was just finishing up its last circuit of the rink, making the surface of the ice smooth and milk-shiny. The crowd wildly applauded the Zamboni driver like he was winning the Daytona 500. Zamboni Driver waved wildly back.

"He has a great job," Hector said. "I'd like to be him."

I stared at the Zamboni as they opened up the big gate doors to let it off the ice. It looked like driving a tractor into a barn.

"You'd like to be him," I said flatly.

At the same time, all the players from both teams began filing onto the ice for the pre-game skate. The crowd went mental.

"Instead of one of *them*," I said, louder but still flat.

He nodded.

"Why?"

He shrugged. "Looks like a really nice job. And all them people treating you nice, treating you really nice, really special, and then you get to leave again without them even knowing who you are. I think that would be great. I think his life would be a nice life."

I stopped watching players loosening up, skating

amazingly tight, quick circles, which was hard to turn away from.

"How sick are you, exactly?" I asked him.

"I'm not that sick. I'll be okay."

"I'm not so sure," I said. "I never knew anybody who dreamed of being a Zamboni driver before."

The two pals, Skitz and Father Mullarkey, made their way back down our row, arms loaded with refreshments, and laughing away. Father came in first, taking the seat beside me, with Skitz on the aisle seat. They started passing stuff down to us: a large Coke, then another, then a giant pretzel, then another. Skitz I could see tucking into the same order, and Father settled in with two pretzels, two tall cups of beer, and one big broad smile.

By the time I had taken my first sip, the good guys had scored, everybody was up and screaming, and we were off to the races.

Except not everybody.

"Are you sure you're all right?" I asked Hector again.

"Look at me," he said. "I got a big Coke and a great big pretzel. Look, I'm eating it too." He took a mouse bite. "See? I'm fine now."

They scored again. Everybody up again. Hector joined us this time, but by the time he got up everybody else was getting down, and by the time he got down, Father was getting up again.

"I'll be back, guys," he said. "Gotta take a squirt."

We all looked back and forth and back at one another. "He said 'squirt,' right?" Skitz said.

"He said 'squirt,'" I said.

"I think we'll keep him," Skitz said.

Hector said nothing.

The Mighty Ducks scored a goal. I was personally embarrassed for the Bruins, and you could feel the depression in the whole building. I told myself it was only one goal. Then the guy who scored did a kind of flamenco dance, and some knucklehead with a duck-billed baseball hat jumped up in front of me and danced along with him. It was still only one goal—but it hurt a lot anyway.

Father Mullarkey returned from his squirt. He had two more beers in his hands, and three bags of potato chips clamped in his teeth. I looked down to find his first two beers nearly empty, but not quite. He drank each down four-fifths of the way before moving on to the next.

Before the first period ended, all the pretzels were gone, all the chips were gone, all the Cokes and four-fifths of the beers. There were two fights, and the Bruins were leading 3–1. The joint was rocking.

"Is this what heaven is like?" I asked Father loudly.

"Exactly like this," he shouted back, "except with non-Caucasian people too."

Then Father left, along with half the people there, to wait in various lines between periods.

"I gotta go to the bathroom," Hector mumbled.

"You should've gone before the period ended," I said. "You'll wait in line forever now."

He was about to say something back, then gagged instead. He bent way over forward, hung there for a few seconds, then made some gurgling, coughing, choking sounds. He covered his mouth and nose with both hands, coughed a bit more.

"That is *so disgusting,* man," Skitz said, bending way down and leaning over to get a better look. I told him to shut his face. Then, as long as he was down there,

Skitz got the bright idea to drain all of Father Mullarkey's not-quite-dead soldiers. He got through the first three in about four seconds.

I was patting Hector on the back with my right hand while taking backhand swings at Skitz with the other. "You better cut that out," I said. "Father will kill you if he catches—"

"I won't kill him," Father said, standing over Skitz now, "but I will do this. . . ." He raised one big hand—the beer-free one, balled in a meaty fist—and dropped it. It fell, like a wrecking ball from the sky, right down onto the back of Skitz's head.

Skitz jerked forward, his face almost bouncing off the seat in front of him. Then he righted himself rigid, and stared up at Father Mullarkey. For his part, Mullarkey looked kind of saintly, with a big soft smile.

"I'm sorry, son, but as I am the shepherd, I must always be aware of the care of my flock. Your well-being is my greatest concern, so I cannot let bad things befall you."

Father rested his hand like a blessing on top of Skitz's head as he climbed over him to get to his seat.

"Ya, well, your punch befalling on the back of my

head was a bad thing."

"In the service of a much greater good," he said. Then he turned to check out Hector, who was just now straightening up again. And looking very pale.

"You all right?" Father asked.

Hector nodded. It was not a convincing nod. He had missed the entire Zamboni performance, and the teams were out again, circling the gleaming ice surface. The sound system was pounding out that *HONK-honk-honk-honk, HONK-honk-honk-honk* tune that was always followed by a mad crowd roar before the action began.

The referee dropped the puck, and we could again hear the cracking of sticks and the cutting of blades into the ice, through the constant growl of the crowd. The buzz was back in my stomach again and I was just leaning forward, leaning farther into the game, when it was all blocked out by the bulk of Father.

"You are not all right," he said, practically lifting Hector out of his seat. He pulled him out, and as he was walking him off, handed me a twenty-dollar bill. "Here's for carfare home, Andrew, and whatever you want for yourselves. I have to take this guy home."

Hector was standing there, dangling at the end of Father's grip like a ventriloquist's dummy, only one that wouldn't talk.

"We'll go too," I said, standing.

Father practically pushed me back down into my seat.

"There's no need for that," he said, like a command. "That would be a waste."

"And waste is a sin," Skitz said helpfully.

Nobody bothered to add to that. Father led Hector away, Hector followed away, and I watched them until they were out the exit.

Skitz scooted over into the seat next to me.

"I hope he's all right," I said.

"Of course he's all right," Skitz said. "He's Hector, man. He's indestructible."

Then he bent down and scooped up the fourth unfinished beer and drained it. "Waste is a sin," he said cheerfully, then picked up the nearly untouched one Father had just put down.

I looked over to the spot where Hector had been hanging his head. On the concrete floor between where his feet were there were three half-dollar-size splotches of what looked an awful lot like blood.

"Get a look at this, Skitz," I said.

He had his head tipped way back as he guzzled down that whole big beer, fast, on top of the several partial beers already sitting in his stomach. I waited.

"Ahhh," he said, refreshed and enlivened like a real beer commercial. Then he dropped the cup and grinned like a chimp.

"Look," I said, and pointed at the splotches.

He leaned across in front of me, examined the stains closer. "W'sat?" he said.

"I think it came out of Hector," I told him.

He stared a few seconds more, and his color changed to something a little gray-greener than usual. Then he sat up, made like he was on top of the hockey game.

He was still grinning when he collapsed forward and bounced off the seat-back in front of him.

I apologized to the guy, who turned around, even though he had that stupid hat on. He scowled at Skitz.

So did I. I collected him up and plunked him hard back into his seat. Unlike with Hector, Skitz's sickness just made me mad. He wavered, but stayed. And he held the same bozo smile he wore on his trip to the floor. Only now, one front tooth was sawed off at an angle like the blade of a guillotine.

Back to the floor for me. I had spent as much time looking at the Garden floor as the ice surface, and that was making me flush with anger as I thought about it.

"Here," I growled at Skitz, shoving the missing puzzle piece of his tooth into his hand. "Now just sit there and shuddup until the Bruins kick the crap out of the Mighty Ducks or I'm gonna do the same to you."

Skitz sat good as gold, the Bruins beat the Ducks 6–4, and I left the Garden feeling rotten as hell. That's a world upside down, that's what that is.

STICKS LIKE
KER-AZEE

I DIDN'T ACTUALLY SEE HECTOR AGAIN UNTIL MONDAY AT school. I thought about him nonstop, however. He didn't even go to Mass on Sunday. God skips Mass more often than Hector does.

"Headaches?"

"Ya, that's right. I get headaches. You don't get headaches?"

"I'm getting one right now, actually. You're giving it to me."

"Well, here you go, then, I got just what you need." He tossed me his handy bottle of St. Joseph aspirin.

"I didn't mean that I actually *had* a headache," I said. I opened the bottle and ate three or four. "And you been eating these to take care of your headaches?"

"Ya. Except when it's bad, and then I take real aspirin."

"When it's bad. What's bad? Like a headache that *bleeds*, is that what you'd call bad?"

"I suppose, I'd call that bad."

"How often would you say it's bad then, Hector?"

"Oh, lemme see . . . oh, right, *shuddup,* that's how often."

"I see. And besides St. Joes and regular aspirin, you eating any other solids these days?"

"You know, Drew, I already got a mother."

"Right. And lots of Fathers."

I must have been really irritated to have been that stupid. That was a Skitz-level thing to say, but I thought Hector told me everything. He used to tell me everything. Now he was coming apart, as far as I could see, and it was throwing off the balance of everything because he was not telling me about it, and so I couldn't do anything about it.

And to make things just that much better, I was starting to mouth off like Skitz, which meant he was going to have to give me a beating like Skitz and I would deserve it like Skitz.

Until we were saved by Skitz.

"Hey, wouldja look? Is this cool? I mean, is this cool? It's cool, and I did it myself, wouldja believe."

Nobody seemed concerned now that I was standing there all squinted and flinched while Hector Subjector held a bunched-up piece of my shirt in one fist and his fist in the other fist, ready to erase me. We could only stare at the Skitzonian Institution, and the thing itself could only stand there beaming.

"I am definitely going to be a dentist now," Skitz said. "And they make lots of dough, don't they. We're all gonna be rich now, guys, because I got a calling, and I'll of course take care of you guys as well. Nobody gets left behind. You could be my assistant, and you could be my accountant." He made no visible indication of which one of us would be which.

It was his tooth. It had reattached itself. Or, as Dr. Fitzsimmons had just said—and as he could not say what he did not mean, we had to believe him—*he* had reattached it.

Not even close to straight. The edges didn't line up. And, it was slightly twisted.

"Ah, nice work, Skitz," Hector said. He let go of me and inched up to check it out. He grasped it between his thumb and finger. He checked it for tightness, first tugging lightly, then harder, then wobbling Skitz's mad grinning head around like a cheerleader's pom-pom.

"How did you do that, Skitz?" I asked.

He didn't even wait to have the foreign fingers out of his mouth. "Kvazey Gvue," he chirped.

"Huh?" I said.

Hector was still amazed, and wouldn't stop pulling at the weird, wrong tooth.

Skitz bit him.

"Ow." Hector pulled back, but didn't retaliate. It was like Skitz had some kind of powers now.

"Krazy Glue," he said serenely. He was acting like he believed his own doctorness, and was giving a lecture. "It really does work. Like that guy on the commercial, and they glue his hard hat to a girder with just one drop and hang him from a building and he dangles there, kicking his legs? And he yells out, 'Sticks like Ker-azee'? Well, it does. It is just that strong. It's a miracle. I'm gonna use it for everything now . . . everything."

I thought of Skitz Fitzsimmons patrolling the world with a great big tube of Krazy Glue, and a chill ran down me.

"I don't think they recommend that, Skitz," I said. "Not for everything."

"Sure they do," he said, and his case was boosted by the gradual arrival of a swarm of curious admirers, kids coming from all corners of the schoolyard to look at the tooth, then touch it, then yank on it.

"Go ahead," Skitz said. "Pull. It'll never come out."

Some people pulled so hard it seemed the front of his skull would come off if the tooth didn't. But everything stayed in place, and Skitz loved it.

Somebody, though, didn't love it.

Shortly before lunchtime, as we sat through Sister trying her holy heart out to convince us that Tom Sawyer wasn't the most ridiculous kid on any river ever, an announcement came over the loudspeaker. It was always a haunt when that thing squawked to life unexpectedly. Between the squelchy screech of the unit turning on, then the faraway tiny version of the secretary's voice coming through, it sounded just the way I always figured a Martian invasion would sound when they finally came to smack us around for all those awful movies.

And it was ten times worse of a haunt when it came with your name attached.

And as is so often the case, my name came with Skitz's attached, and Hector's. We were to take our bag lunches across the yard to the church basement, where we were to have an audience with the chief.

"Ooooo-ooooooo!" The whole class taunted us, and I know they are supposed to say that at times like these, and I know I would be ooo-oooing as loud as anyone, but that didn't make them not jerks. They were jerks.

"Jerks," I said loud as the bell rang for lunch. Of course, that's just what they want, and they oooed louder and laughed louder. I turned to notice Skitz was right in there with them, ooo-oooing until Hector cuffed him in the back of the head.

"Oh, right," Skitz said, "it's us."

"What do they want us for?" I said as we were halfway across the yard, clutching our brown bags so hard that whatever the lunches were they would all look the same when we opened them.

"Maybe Hector won another award," Skitz said, fingering his tooth.

"Right," I said. "And they want to keep it a secret, so it's at lunchtime in the church basement."

It was like trying sarcasm on a happy dog.

"Right," Skitz said. "And why are we going?"

"They need somebody to clap," I said, running out of steam.

Hector said not a word. He was looking the church building up and down like it was a deeply untrustworthy character. He looked like he was headed to the gallows.

"Oh, come on, man. 'Sokay. It couldn't be *that* bad." I put a hand on his shoulder. He brushed it away gently.

I could be wrong sometimes. From the first appearance when we walked through the heavy basement door, you'd have to conclude this was one of those times. We were greeted—and that is a very questionable use of the term—by not one, but a whole trinity of the Franchise. The firm of Blarney, Mullarkey, and Shenanigan, a symphony in black.

And yes, they were all in black. Father Mullarkey was there, looking grim and somber and more like a priest than I had ever seen him. Couldn't be good.

"Sit down, boys," Monsignor Blarney said, and it was no invitation.

We lined up on a wooden bench that sat under a window on the street side of the church. When he gestured at our lunch bags with that rolling *Get on with it, get on with it* gesture, we dug in.

"We don't have a long time for this, and so I will get right to the matter while you eat. The question, as you probably already know, is, what happened?"

We were all just starting to chew when we all stopped again.

Skitz went automatic. "Nothing happened, Father, I swear."

"Monsignor," Monsignor snapped.

"Nothing happened, Monsignor, I swear. It wasn't us. Ask anybody. I swear."

"Stop saying that, Mr. Fitzsimmons. Stop swearing."

"But I didn't swear, Father, I swear. Drew, did I—?"

"*Fitzsimmons!*" Monsignor barked. He let his

mouth hang open but then seemed to lose enthusiasm as he thought about the many different Skitticisms he had to correct. So he just turned away from him with a *hmmmph* of disgust.

"He wants to know about the other night," Father Mullarkey said. "The Bruins game." He wasn't speaking in his usual confident and boisterous way.

I had a mouthful of tuna, but the question seemed to be addressed to me. "Bruins won, six to four," I said.

Skitz had now caught the interest of Father Shenanigan. Father came right up close and lifted Skitz's chin to look at him, at his dentistry. "So it's true, then," he said, and then he roughly sort of tossed Skitz's face away like he wished he could throw his whole head. "My God, lad, you're an idiot."

"That's enough," Monsignor said, and came up to Skitz. "What happened to your tooth?" he asked him.

Skitz grinned helplessly. "I glued it, Father. It's amazing. Go on, pull it. There's nothing you can do."

"Call the monsignor Monsignor," Father Mullarkey said, pleadingly.

Monsignor went on, "What I meant was, how did you break the tooth?"

Suddenly I saw the questions. I saw them forming an orderly line.

"He fell," I blurted.

"Eat your lunch, Mr. St. Cyr," Shenanigan said. "We will speak to you in your turn."

I ate.

"I fell," Skitz said. "Like Mister St. Cyr said."

He turned and gave me a smile and a nod. God help us, please Skitz, keep it simple.

"You find something funny, Mr. Fitzsimmons?" Shenanigan said.

"No, Father."

"Then just tell Monsignor about when you fell."

"I fell at the game."

"Why should you fall at the game?" Monsignor asked.

"I don't really like blood," Skitz said.

"Was there blood in the hockey game?"

"There's always blood in a hockey game," Hector cut in. The sound of his voice now, because he was so silent, was alarming. He had stopped chewing too, so his end of the bench was eerie calm.

"Ya, but this was Hector's blood, made me woozy."

That orderly line I was talking about? With the questions? Skitz never sees those kind of things.

"I see," said Monsignor in a low, thoughtful voice. "Now, this is the thing. We had a visit from Hector's mother, who we all know well and who is a wonderful, wonderful lady. And she came to us concerned, about Saturday night. Her son came home sick, as I believe you all know."

"Yes, Monsignor," the three of us said, though Skitz said "Father."

"And, well, she was concerned that Hector was dropped off—dropped off, left at his door—sick that evening. And he continued to be unwell the next morning and throughout most of Sunday. We all missed him at the Masses, which was highly unusual."

"Sorry, Monsignor," Hector said.

Monsignor waved him off. "And add to that, that Mr. Fitzsimmons here had what appears to be a nasty mishap with his tooth. It all adds up to a spectacularly unfortunate Altar Boy of the Year celebration, doesn't it?"

"The Bruins won, Monsignor," I said, "six to four."

He let out an angry sigh. Monsignor Blarney's angry

sigh carries about the same force as a Doberman's growl.

"Oh, for God's sake, boys," Father Shenanigan yelled. "Was there any drinking going on at this game Saturday night?"

Uh-oh.

"Of course there was," Skitz blurped. "It was a Bruins game at the Garden."

"I mean," Shenanigan growled now, "were *you* boys drinking any alcohol that night?"

"Of course not," I said as quick as I could say it, to head off you-know-who. "We're not old enough for that, Father."

"No, of course you're not. So did anybody provide alcohol for you?"

"I didn't buy them any beers," Father Mullarkey said flatly.

"Nobody drank anything," Hector said. He was hunched forward, looking straight ahead. He looked like that statue, *The Thinker*, if *The Thinker* had his brown-bag lunch crushed in his hand.

"So what did you have that made you sick?" Father Shenanigan pressed him.

"Nothing. I had a bite of a pretzel. And a Coke."

"And why did you faint, Fitzsimmons?"

Skitz wasn't catching on, exactly, but he knew enough to be getting uncomfortable.

"I had the same. Pretzel and Coke."

"Me too," I said, though nobody asked.

"So why did you faint?" Monsignor wanted to know.

"It was the blood, like I said. Only, I didn't faint."

"There was no blood," Shenanigan snapped, running both hands back over his grease-head. "It was beer."

"I think I can tell the difference between blood and beer, Father. Now, if it was blood and wine you were talking about—"

"Fitzsimmons!" Shenanigan, out of patience, rushed Skitz now. He had rushed him before, but when you see it, you can tell the difference between rushing a guy and *rushing* a guy, and Shenanigan's big long bones in motion fill a room like a giant angry rabid bat.

Father Mullarkey shoved right up and got between them. He stood, hulking up to Shenanigan, who didn't seem at all intimidated. "Just ask your questions,"

Father Mullarkey said.

He pushed past. "You drank beer on Saturday night, Mr. Fitzsimmons, didn't you?"

Lie, Skitz, I prayed. I honest-to-God prayed for a lie, right there. For once do the smart thing and take care of yourself. And, while you're at it . . .

It was as if Shenanigan heard my prayer, which I suppose they are capable of in certain circumstances. He had to see my prayer and raise me one. "And you know lying only gets you in deeper, with us and with God. The truth will eventually come out, and a stack of lies will be a much more serious affair. There is no such thing as a single lie."

I didn't even have hope at this point.

"I drank beer," he said solemnly.

"You see," Father Shenanigan said, wheeling around to show us his back as he addressed Monsignor. "There was no blood, Monsignor. It was alcohol made these boys sick. There was nothing wrong with Hector but corruption. He is a perfectly healthy boy when not being interfered with." He shot Father Mullarkey a look.

"I never drank any alcohol in my life," Hector said. "Not once."

"Where did you get the beer?" Monsignor asked Skitz.

"Off the floor."

"Oh, for God's sake," said Shenanigan.

"I never drank no beer," Hector insisted.

"Where did the beer *come* from?" Monsignor asked in a patient-but-running-out tone.

Skitz is prone to spasms. Not, for the most part, medical-muscular-type spasms, though he can have those too. But spasms of pretty much every other kind. Like honesty, stupidity, and obnoxiousness. Like spitting, like sharpening brand-new pencils down until they're ground to nothing. Like loudness and quietness and warmth. Like wildness and melancholy and humor. He is, at any given moment, likely to be in the grip of one spasm or another, and often several at once even if they would not seem to go together, like generosity and hate. And the thing is, being spasms, they come at you from nowhere and can completely reverse how things were just going previously, like now when he was hit with a spasm of daredevil and understanding and loyalty.

"I'm not telling you," Skitz said. He said it softly,

but it was like someone had hauled the Liberty Bell into the room and gave it an almighty bong.

"What did you say?" Shenanigan growled.

The school bell, sounding just like a fire alarm, clanged out in the yard for the end of lunch. Monsignor came on like a man who did not have time to waste.

"Did Father Mullarkey buy you beer, Mr. Fitzsimmons?"

"No, he did not."

"Then where did you get the beer, and God help you if you lie to me."

"I won't lie to you. But with all due respect, I won't truth to you either."

If ever a situation was made for the phrase *Holy hell*, this was that moment. Everybody in the room was thinking it, for sure. Nobody would be saying it, however.

"The lunch bell rang, Monsignor," I said. Nice try, huh?

"You will leave when I tell you to leave. Mr. Fitzsimmons, I will ask you one more time: Who provided you with the alcohol?"

"I'm afraid I'm going to have to take the Fifth

Commandment on this one, Monsignor."

Father Mullarkey coughed out a short, barky laugh. "You're a good boy, Skitz, honoring your father and mother."

"Well, I'd honor him if I knew where he was. I'd honor him with my good sharp pencil, right in his big fat neck—"

"I think he means the Fifth Amendment, Monsignor," I blurted.

"I know what he means, and it means nothing here. But here is something that does have meaning: this school, with its fine record of achievement, is very popular to the point of being oversubscribed. We are in a position to be very selective about who is in and who is out. You want to be in, not out, Mr. Fitzsimmons. The world will not be a very accommodating place for the likes of you, I can tell you that. Outside of the nurturing environment of a place like Blessed Sacrament, you would have a very rough ride indeed. How would you like to find yourself on a bus every morning instead of taking your casual stroll from two blocks up the road? How do you like the idea of being bused across to Mattapan for the rest of your school life? How does that sound?"

"I don't know anybody in Mattapan, Monsignor," Skitz said, and he said it in a voice half his size. He said it in a sadness I did not recognize, and it made me want to just reach over and hang on to him. But I couldn't do that.

But Hector could. In a move that was both silent and audacious, he got up from his end of the bench, walked past me, and sat on the other side of Skitz, right up close to him. We had a solidarity sandwich.

Monsignor stared uncomprehendingly, then pressed on. "Well, I do know Mattapan," he said, "and you wouldn't like it. You are on a slippery slope, young man, and something is going to come of it. You are headed in the wrong direction."

"I can change," he said, still that sad guy. This was really bothering him, the thought of getting shipped out. "I can change direction. Directions can change."

Father Shenanigan chose then to throw his two cents into the collection plate. "No, they can't. Not when they are downhill."

"I'm not downhill," Skitz snapped.

"Tell me," Monsignor said, "did anyone say anything when you came home drunk with a broken tooth on Saturday?"

"I did not come home drunk."

"Did anyone say anything?"

"No."

Shenanigan located another two cents. "Hnn," he sniffed. "I don't wonder."

There they let it hang, like they had achieved some kind of point. The room filled up with clammy silence. It was wicked uncomfortable and only highlighted the fact that the biggest two silences were the biggest two presences, Hector and Father Mullarkey, who were now seeming to shrink into themselves, the opposite of the way they normally filled a place up.

Monsignor waited until the tension reached just to breaking point before he released it.

"You are going to have to get back to class," he said, as if this disappointed him. "I am going to give you each a last chance: Did Father Mullarkey provide you with beer? Now, regardless of what you tell me at this point, it will not be held against you. You will not be punished for what you tell me now—we just need to get to the truth." He let his generosity set in, took a long breath. "So. Did Father—"

Left to right: "No," snapped Hector. "No," snapped Skitz. "No," snapped I.

"Then who did?"

We did the only thing we could do. We stared straight ahead, looked him in the eyes, and didn't say anything.

Monsignor's whole head went red in an instant, accentuating his shocky white hair and making him look like a flaming torch.

"Return to class," he rumbled.

He did *not* have to repeat himself this time.

DIVIDE AND CONQUER

THERE'S NEVER A GOOD TIME FOR CONFESSION. BUT sometimes the time is *so* bad it makes you certain there is a God.

It was another part of the ongoing drive to get us to our Confirmation, earning us the Gifts of the Holy Spirit and certifying us as Soldiers in Christ. It had never occurred to me that Christ would need soldiers, or that he'd be the military commander type, but I guess that's why I was here to be educated.

We were sitting in the front pews, stage left of the humongous church, made all the more humongous by the fact that our Confirmation class was the only group in the place. This was uncomfortable enough under regular circumstances, on a Saturday when anybody from the parish or even outside it was welcome. At least then you could try and blend in with the population at large. With a little mumbling and voice warp you might be able to pass yourself off as one of the old-folk Confession groupies who were always there waiting when they opened up shop, even if they didn't appear to have the strength to commit a sin, or one of the older teenagers who were hoping to commit some that night and wanted to get their booster shot. But here, now, just twenty-six little boot-campers for the Army of the Lord matched up with the two priests who had spent months preparing them for that very same Confirmation? What were the chances he wouldn't know who we were when we were in there? They were not supposed to know, they were just supposed to be God's switchboard operators and not listen in.

Skitz Fitz was squirming more than usual. He had been squirming since the moment Monsignor suggested shipping him out.

"Do you think they'll do it, Drew? Do you think they're gonna send me to Mattapan?"

"C'mon, Skitz, we've always known it's just a matter of time. You're going to Mattapan."

Mattapan was famous, for one thing. It was so renowned for the old state mental hospital there, lots of people weren't even aware there was an actual town wrapped around it. Nine times out of ten, when somebody just used the word *Mattapan* they were referring to what the old-timers called "The Mattapan Nuthouse," and it didn't even matter that the place had been closed for years. If somebody said you were going to be put in Mattapan, it meant you were officially mental.

"This is serious, Drew. I can't go anyplace without you guys. Monsignor Jerkwad was right—I won't make it on the outside."

Jerkwads though they be, this was their thing. They knew stuff, the priests. They knew stuff about you that you didn't expect them to know. I don't know if the seminary over there in Brighton had some special Department of Getting Inside Poor Chumps' Heads and Then Screwing Them Up with It, but somehow their graduates had a knack for doing just that. I had to give them credit.

Wait. No, I didn't.

"He doesn't know what he's talking about, Skitz. He was trying to scare you. And since you are known for lacking the normal human sense of fear, he had to try anything and everything to get at you."

"Well it worked. He's at me."

A girl came out of the far-side confessional. Looked like she was going to cry, except for the streaks of joy and excitement slashing across her newly liberated face. That's the Confession experience for you, right there. We all scooted down one space closer to the inevitable.

Skitz was next up.

"You don't know, Drew. You don't know what they're doing to me."

"Sure I do. They do it to everybody."

"Drew, they do it to me more, and you know it. And they are turning up the heat. They're messing me up. Saying I shouldn't even be making my Confirmation, saying I'm not *God-fearing* enough. What's that supposed to mean?"

"Well, first, should that be a good thing? Should that be the point? What kind of a God wants you to be afraid of him? And second, I don't think you have anything to worry about there, Skitz, because I'm sure God is much more afraid of you than you are of him."

While this high-level discussion of God and fear and Skitz was going on, something quieter and probably much higher was going on, up at the altar rail. Hector. Hector had already done his Confession, anxious as he was to get to the head of the line ahead of everybody, anxious as he always is to get to the head of the Confession line. Hector treated the Confession line the way most people treated the ice cream man line, and when Hector wants something, folks around here usually give it to him, and when *anybody* wants your spot in Confession line, you usually give it to him. Not that it comes up that often.

But what was really unusual here was the time Hector was spending on his knees at the altar rail. Normally, the time Hector is required to spend at the altar praying away his sins is less than the time it takes him to walk the distance from the confessional. While he does not divulge details, I have clocked him in the past, and unless he's been to an Evelyn Wood speed-praying course, they must tell him to say about a quarter of a Hail Mary and maybe throw in the first six words of the Our Father.

But that wasn't this time.

In between things, between calming Skitz and worrying myself, coming up with believable-yet-not-too-provocative sins to confess and pretending that it all wasn't even happening, I kept flicking back to Hector up there at the altar rail. On the wrong side of the altar rail. In every respect, Hector Fossas had the right to be on the other side of that particular holy fence, lording it over the ordinary citizens who were here at church because they wanted to be good, but were out in the audience with the common riffraff because they weren't all *that* good. Hector Fossas *was* that good, whether he wanted to be up there as Altar Boy of the Year or Father Fossas or Jesus' long-lost brother—it was his call—because, for my money, that's how good a guy he was. Better guy than me, that's for sure.

But there he was, on his knees with his back to the crowd, doing his penance. And doing it. And doing it. Six, seven, eight other kids popped out of the confessional, went up to the rail, Pennanced themselves spotless, and left Hector still there. It gave me the shakes, and I was surely not the only one to notice. What was

Father Shenanigan doing to him? What was he telling him in there, what was he making him think? How could he justify putting Hector on the rail like that, because I can tell you, it wasn't for sins. It wasn't for honest-to-God sins committed by Hector Fossas, uh-uh.

So when he was finally wrapping up, getting to his feet and crossing himself, kissing his scapular and bowing to the massive Christ statue altarpiece, you could feel a sigh of relief ease up out of the whole class because things were something like right again.

Until he threw us for an even bigger loop. Instead of turning right and right again to walk behind the altar, toward the sacristy and out the door back to class, Hector turned left. He came right back down, got to the far end of the pew, and took his seat at the end of the line.

He was going back for more.

"What the hell?" Skitz said at the sight of it.

"I don't know," I said. "Even you couldn't commit another sin in between your confession and your penance."

"Not true exactly," he said. "Once I had my hand in

my pocket on my way back, and there's a big hole in the pocket—"

"I don't want to know," I said, putting my hand up in front of his face. The confessional opened up, spitting out another poor sap and creating a space for the next one, Skitz. "Don't tell me," I said, nudging him out of the pew. "Tell him."

He stood there, making a small spectacle. "I hate telling him. I hate telling any of them anything. They always abuse me something wicked."

"Shuddup ya baby, a few Hail Marys is not abuse."

"No, it isn't, but I get the Hail Marys after they abuse me first. It's like a little torture chamber in there."

"You're imagining it. Just go, and get it over with."

"Oh ya?" he said, and before I knew it he had grabbed my tie and was yanking me along behind him.

"I can't do this," I said.

"Shh," he said, pulling me hard and serious. His face was desperate and sad and pleading and threatening to create a scene that would pull us both into a hole of punishment and humiliation that we'd never climb out of. I was better off going along.

Which was amazing, considering. Considering this was a Skitz plan. Considering the half dozen or so classmates left in the pews behind us were potential witnesses. Giggling, muttering witnesses.

Considering I was actually smuggling into the confessional box *with* another guy, and that had to be some kind of record, sinning and confessing simultaneously, creating an unsolvable perpetual black hole of sin, resulting in the breaking of probably millions of church laws.

Not to mention the breaking of millions of our bones, if we got caught.

They can see the shadow of you, of course. When you are in there, when it is your turn and the priest in the middle booth swings around from the person in the opposite cubicle to address you, he slides open his small window and reveals a silhouette of his big priest head there. So then he can see about the same amount of you. It's part of what makes it so eerie and intimidating, that and the whispering. I could actually see the outlines of the ends of his wide, slick mustache stretching beyond the trace of his face.

So I had to be a shadow. I had to be a shadow of a

shadow, sliding myself right in behind Skitz, crouched and clamped to him as he knelt there waiting for Father Shenanigan to address him. And I had to make surely sure I made no sound or movement that set me apart from the guy who was actually supposed to be in there.

I nearly blew it right out of the chute when Father shushed open the little sliding window. It sounded to me like a train speeding past my head, then slamming into a wall. I let out a gasp. If Father noticed, he didn't show it. Probably he got a lot of that, gasping.

"Bless me, Father, for I have sinned," Skitz began. "It has been four months since my last confession."

"Seven," Father said.

Oh jeez. Hell, did I wish I wasn't in that booth.

"Sorry, Father, maybe it was seven. Right, where was . . . Right, it has been . . ." I could just about hear the workings of his brain, partly because my ear was pressed right up against it, partly because his brain was doing just what my brain was doing. Once you get knocked off of that *Bless me, Father* track, it's a real scramble to get back on.

". . . And *these* are my sins," Skitz finally announced, so pleased to be back in shape he sounded like he was introducing guests on *The Tonight Show*. "I lied, I stole, I swore. . . ." I could almost have delivered the list in his place, since he was working from the standard sheet. How are you supposed to remember every slip you made over the last four months or seven months? You couldn't do it. You had to fall back on the standards and hope they sounded convincing enough. But of course if you were Skitz Fitzsimmons, standard couldn't ever stay standard. I don't know if he deviated from the script to be a wise guy or just because his mind wandered off, but deviate he did.

"And I had a provolone-cheese-and-mortadella sandwich that I brought into church. And I farted loud during Mass—because of the sandwich—and made people laugh."

"That is not a sin," Father said tersely.

"Oh, and I had some really freaky thoughts."

"Those are not—"

"Maybe you should hear what they were first—"

"Shush," Father Shenanigan said. That was the first time I ever heard that in the confessional. That was the first time I ever heard *of* that in the confessional. A guy tries to confess, in the confessional, and they tell him not to bother? But it didn't amount to abuse, like Skitz said, and in fact you couldn't really even blame him, since I pretty seriously wanted Skitz to shush the hell up myself.

"But I didn't get to tell you about what I did in the bathtub. . . ."

Father sighed. Not a big deal, right? And in light of Skitz's determination to cough up details of stuff that would make God wince, not even unreasonable, was it?

Except it was. It was something. If a sigh could ever be described as a pukey sigh, this was the one. Father had leaned himself way forward, let his forehead press against the frame of the screen between them, and he sighed, fat and dramatic and unmistakable, right at Skitz. It was a sigh that said, Your sins, kid, and your weird thoughts and your feelings are wasting my time. You are not a project worth the effort. And I can't even see any reason to try and hide that fact from you.

And that, after all, was the abuse part. Promised, delivered.

But Father Shenanigan had no faith in Skitz to understand a message, so he drove it home.

"For God's sake, will you just shut up, boy."

Skitz already knew that's what the man meant, because he had already stopped. He stopped talking, he stopped trying. He stopped sweating, even, because I could feel everything the way the front of me was pressed up against the back of him. His racey-pacey heartbeat dropped to about half its regular speed, down somewhere between jackrabbit and humming-bird.

"Say three Hail Marys," Father said distractedly, "and three Our Fathers. . . ."

And then the two of them together mumboed the jumbo, *In the name of The Father, and of The Son.* . . .

Skitz and I were very careful, very good, working as one to stand together, cast one shadow, make no fuss. We were very much like one being, which shouldn't have been that surprising, since I think Skitz and Hector and I all together could practically pull it off, the way we were together. Skitz pulled the curtain to finally get us loose. And expose us to the light.

"Andrew," Father growled, awakening thirty mil-lion bats in my stomach, "as long as you're here . . ."

Skitz didn't even turn. He ran, out of the booth and down the side aisle toward school. He forgot to even go to the altar rail to say his penance. Probably just a formality anyway.

I pulled the curtain closed again, knelt back down, the bats clawing my stomach and my head in a spin. Father slowly closed the sliding wooden partition as he went to deal with the person on the other side and let me stew in my own sweaty juices. I listened to the low murmur of the other confession and squirmed more than you would have thought possible in a two-by-two box. There was more total perspiration now, and more heartbeats per minute, than when there were two knuckleheads squeezed in here together.

After about six years of that, the small door slid open again.

"Bless me, Father, for I have sinned. . . ," I started, and did not stop. I confessed to all the usual suspects, and every other thing I could think of. I was a filthy and depraved but contrite little swine. I was sorry for everything, and I sounded sorry because scared out of your mind usually sounds quite like sorry when it comes out of your mouth. I made the Act of Contrition sound like "Those Lazy Hazy Crazy Days of Summer," which was simultaneously running through my head and only didn't come out because, thank God, Father put me out of my misery at last.

"Mr. St. Cyr," Father said flatly. "Your litany of sins is disturbing, no question. More worrisome still, however, is your habit of placing yourself at the center of business that is not necessarily yours. You may make a fine priest someday, but you are not one now. Believe it or not, there are persons in this parish even better qualified than you to care for the spiritual needs of others. You are not the Father around here."

A big fat stupid part of me wanted to debate the point. The thin, smart part won out.

"Yes, Father."

"Hubris, son, is the root of as much evil as money ever was. Do bear that in mind, before it becomes your personal demon."

As soon as I found out what hubris was, I would bear it in mind.

"I will, Father."

"Now, for all your sins, of omission as well as commission, as well as the outrage of having sat in on another confession—which, were it any *other* confession, would have resulted in even more severe action—

you will say one entire rosary . . ."

Wow. I had never done a whole rosary before. That would eat up at least another entire class. Unintended bonus.

". . . during your lunch hour . . ."

Should've known. Fair enough.

". . . and another two complete rosaries, here at the altar, after school."

That was an ecclesiastical ass-whipping, right there.

For which, of course, I thanked him. "Thank you, Father." We mumboed the jumbo together, and then I opened that curtain and got out for real.

By the time I did, the whole rest of the class had done the duty, got through it, and got back to class. Monsignor—who was famously fast and furious at this, only occasionally interrupting your sins to say, "Well, why did you do *that*?"—had already closed up shop on his station and gone off to the rectory to watch game shows and home shopping, which I imagine is what they like to watch.

The only one left was Hector, up there at the rail all over again, praying his guts out.

HABITS OF CREATURES

MY HOUSE WAS ALWAYS A PRIEST-FREE ZONE compared to other places. The biggest reason for that was that the Fathers were always inclined to be coming along and attempting to fill the most obvious Father-shaped holes in the lives of parish families. But in my case, unlike a lot of other houses I knew of, my Father-shaped hole was already filled, by my father.

My hulking, snorting, smoke-billowing, rip-roaring, two-fisted, Church-loathing father.

Don't get me wrong. He left me entirely alone, so I had nothing to fear from the man. Unless I came through the door wearing a black suit with a white dog collar. Then I'd find my face in the blender on my way to becoming a priestshake. Like a lot of old veterans of war and Catholic school, he never talked about whatever horrors turned him so hard-boiled and feisty. But they made a man out of him, and why the hell should I have it any easier?

The undeniable upside was that I didn't have to live with the constant threat of having a man of the cloth rapping at my door, attempting to inject his version of righteous into the family.

I knew of lots of other families who had to live with that. Some of them liked it, even. Some of them didn't. Skitz never liked it. He and his family were a work in progress for the Church practically from day one. What with Skitz coming from frog spawn or something, there was never even a sniff of a dad to the place, so the Fathers were in his house on a regular basis, checking on him, on his mother, on the couple of older Skitzes who lived there up until not too long ago but were now out in the great wide open where such teenagers go once they get big and strong enough to muscle their way out. One Father would show up, day or night but more often night, bringing a pizza once in a while but just as likely expecting to sit down to a quickly slapped-up meal. When I say "all the time," I mean there was a Father there *all* the time in the old days, or at least that's how it seemed to Skitz and to me. That's when it all started—"The Nocturnals," we called them—when Skitz would show up at my window in the middle of the night because he hated listening to the sound of soft priestly murmurings from his bed the way most people would hate listening to the sound of rats running the place.

The visitations tailed off a bit when the first Skitz cleared out, and then when the second one beat it a few months ago, the appearances of black suits at the door decreased dramatically. Skitz was overjoyed and never even considered the possibility of being insulted by the lack of any interest in him as an individual. Though, according to him, his mother sure did. She got way blue over it, as a matter of fact, and wondered out loud what she might have done to put Father off coming. She felt guilty. On the rare occasion something still prompts a visit out of the blue, Skitz peels wallpaper from the walls with his fingernails, and his mom buzzes around the place like St. Peter himself was gracing her with his presence.

See, she wanted what they were supposed to be giving. She wanted what they were all along pretending to be giving, when really they were giving her not much of anything at all. Because Mrs. Fitzsimmons was a good holy simple woman, she expected priests to bring all good things to her house, and to bring them forever. She wouldn't have known they were there to take a lot more than they ever brought, and to finish when there was pretty much nothing left.

They never called once they left, Skitz's brothers. When they were gone, they were gone.

But whether the visitors came or not, Skitz was into The Nocturnals. He had developed a habit, and it suited him down to the ground, wandering the netherworld netherhours. So my window continued to take its share of rapping.

Which was just as well, since while the visitations were declining at the Fitzsimmons homestead, they were coincidentally increasing at the Fossas estate. And mostly that was a welcome thing, what with the Fossases being Supermondocatholics and all, and any Father who came to his door, Hector said, was treated like royalty. So, of course, they all did it at one time or another, because even normal people would find it hard to resist a little worship here and there, and the priests pretty much survive on it.

But even before things got tricky in Hector's family setup, I could see him bending a little at the heaviness of it all. The range of pastoral interest in him and his people narrowed, but the intensity of it increased. Great things were expected of him, all things were expected of him. Then, when his dad pulled the stopper out and let all hell loose, well, I think that was where it all started getting to be too much for the big guy.

I wasn't even giving it a lot of thought anymore, when I went to bed, whether or not I would be woken up by one of the woodpeckers rap-rapping at my window. It seemed as likely that I would be up at three, for a walk and a talk, as I would at six, to start hauling newspapers around. I was getting a little tired, though, most days by lunchtime, and I was starting to wonder if I might have to say no once in a while.

Tap-tap.

Up I was. I went straight to the window, pulled back the curtain to reveal the most unsurprising sight of Skitz Fitzsimmons's demented little face. But it was even more demented than usual, the eyes bugging out like Wile E. Coyote spying the Road Runner with a gun. As he waved at me over and over to come out—as if I thought he was there to deliver my mail or something rather than disturb my sleep and whatever else he could disturb—he also gestured to a spot about ten feet behind him, where Father Mullarkey was standing casually on the sidewalk. Father smiled and waved at me like he was five.

I could hardly skip this session, could I?

"Hi," I said to the two of them when I got outside. It was a cold night, a crystal-clear night, the kind that makes you look right up into the sky when you get out no matter how many times you have seen this, no matter how little there is to actually see up there with the city light half blocking your view.

"Hi," Father said.

Skitz didn't say hi. He wore that same alarmed expression on his face, as if Father Mullarkey had taken him hostage.

"I found this guy on your lawn," Father said.

"He found me on your *lawn*," Skitz repeated.

Everyone seemed to think there was something

shocking about everybody else, without seeing any-thing out of place with themselves, as we stood in front of my house well after midnight on a cold winter week-night.

At the risk of doing the same thing myself, I had to say I was fine, but these guys were not.

Father smiled like a kindly guy, like a guy older than he was. His eyes were glassy, his manner slow and soft. Skitz was his opposite—edgy, bouncing foot-to-foot, eyes likewise wet, but much more worried-looking. This was all very Skitz-*like*, but it was more. It was more than usual, and it was off. Off his regular off. Between the two of them, they gave me a distinctly off-balance feeling, like one of them was trying to speed up the spin of the world and the other one was trying to slow it down and I was trying to keep my footing on top.

"How would you like to go to the diner?" Father said, instead of faking any normal conversation. "For clam strips. Or with bellies, if you prefer."

Nobody likes clam strips more than I do, but God, not the bellies. I had never experienced a stoned priest before, and I was fairly sure I was experiencing one now. So the circumstances of the offer made me think twice.

Skitz didn't even think once. "Let's go," he said, instantly losing the air of suspicion that surrounded him only seconds before. If it appeared that Skitz Fitzsimmons's decision-making process was not unlike that of a bony stray dog, then appearances did not deceive.

"Let's go get Hector," I said.

"Is that necessary?" Father asked.

"Yes, it is," I said.

"No, it isn't," Skitz said. "Hector's getting to be a big drag. He won't want to go. Father M. can be Hector for now."

"Shuddup, Skitz," I said, and started walking in the direction of Hector's place. "We already got a Hector. His name is Hector. This is the deal. If we're out on Nocturnals, we offer him to come. If he doesn't want to that's fine, but we're offering."

I kept walking, and they came along. As if there was some kind of time gap, like we were communicating by walkie-talkie, Skitz said, in a bit, "Right, you're right."

And Father said, in another bit, "I'm not supposed to go there."

I half turned to him but kept on walking. "Huh?"

"I'm not supposed to go there, to the Fossases."

"And what?" I said, gesturing with open hands at the big wide cold nocturnal world around us. "You're supposed to do this?"

"Street ministry," he said. "That's kind of my bag. I don't work the same way the others do, and that is tolerated. To an extent. But Hector Fossas is Father Shenanigan's project. I'm told I'm a bad influence there and I'm to steer far away from Hector."

"What?" Skitz said, suddenly back to nervous Skitz. "So you're not a bad influence here?" He pointed at himself with both pointers.

Now I turned all the way around, to watch Father's reaction while I kept walking backward down the sidewalk.

He didn't say anything right off. His face did, though. He gave Skitz a kind of crumpled look, a smile, a wince, an apology face. He looked embarrassed and sorry for all of us. He shrugged.

"Maybe we're both considered misfits of a sort," Father said warmly.

Skitz didn't look too pleased, though he couldn't

possibly have been truly surprised. "Freaks seek freaks, I guess," Skitz said, answering shrug with shrug.

Father brightened. "Hey," he said. "I like that. I like that very much. You mind if I use that?"

This, I could tell you, was about as big as compliments got in Skitz's world. "Sure," he said, puffing up. "It is pretty good, isn't it? Freaks seek freaks. Make sure you give me credit, though."

"I'll make sure," Father said.

We turned the corner onto Hector's street, and the mood quickly darkened. There, under the streetlight directly in front of Hector's house, sat Father Shenanigan's big fat maroon Cadillac.

All three of us stopped flat-footed in the middle of the sidewalk.

"That's that, then," Father said.

"It is," Skitz said. "That. That is. It's that. It is very much that."

I took a deep breath. "Well, it isn't that. It can't be that. Sorry, but . . . it's the deal. We're not leaving him behind like this, uh-uh."

"I really must not be here," Father Mullarkey said. "This would not be good, for me to be here."

"Just give me a minute," I said. "I'll be right back."

I continued on alone to the house, went down the very narrow walkway between Hector's and the next house where if you reached out your full wingspan you could practically touch both places at once.

I tap-tap-tapped on his window. I waited about ten seconds. Nothing. I tapped again, the way we were supposed to, the way we always did it. Nothing. I waited twenty seconds this time and tapped the third tap, which would be the last tap because that's how it worked, three.

And I waited. I waited even longer than we would normally wait, because, just because. Because I didn't like it. And then I went and did it, I went and blew all the rules right out by knocking a fourth time and didn't even care if I woke Hector up out of the soundest sleep ever and he promised to kill me in the morning. I'd go away from that window and look happily forward all night to getting killed.

But I wasn't going to have that to look forward to. Nothing. He wasn't coming to that window.

It wasn't with any great enthusiasm that the three of us walked the mile and a half toward the bright yellow neon sign of the diner. It was open all night, and so tended to attract an eye-catching cross section of society, which didn't bother Father one bit and seemed to get Skitz pretty excited about the place, and they both wanted to sit right down and eat. Not me, though. The second we stepped in there into the flood of light that was always there but suddenly felt like a bright and burning oppressive light, I wanted to get right back out again.

"Can we take it to go?" I said, and I could see in Father's face that he would have no problem with that.

"Where would you want to go, though?"

I knew where I would want to go, and so did Skitz.

"We got a place," I said.

"We got a place," Skitz said. And he scurried off to the bathroom while Father Mullarkey ordered clam strips and onion rings and Cokes and one order of fried whole clams with disgusting oozing pus-filled bellies that you had to be seriously mentally incorrect to find appetizing.

"My Lord," Father said as he surveyed our spot.

There wasn't much left in the way of food by the

time we got there, but my bag had enough crumb action left to make it still seem like munching. I smiled at Father's reaction, as if I had personally built the Pulpit Elm.

"This is remarkable," he said, mounting the steps slowly, as if he didn't trust them, touching all the bits of tree on his way up to test the reality of it all. And it all creaked with the weight of him. "It's remarkable," he added, when he was up in preaching position out over the river.

"Ya," I said, "it is." Not only was it great like it was always great, it was great in the way it fit Father Mullarkey, and the way he fitted it. I could imagine him being the actual guy who built it, who came up with the idea and laid it all in with his own big mitts, and who preached from it.

I wished Hector was there to see it. He would have felt the same way. He would have felt the rightness of it, and the pride. I should have gotten him out. Even if he was sleeping or whatever, I should have got him out. I should never have left him behind.

Skitz, of course, headed straight down to the water. I took a seat on the steps of the elm while Father stayed up there commanding the ship.

"This is where the church should be," he said. "Right out here. This is where God lives, in places like this, where He wants you to come out and look at what He made for you, and listen to it and love it. He's really just a big kid like that, God is."

I couldn't imagine that this was approved wording straight from the Catholic High Command. But then again, lots of what Father Mullarkey said seemed to stray from the assigned text. Which was lots of all right by me.

"Maybe you should open up your own branch of the Franchise," I said to him. "I'd sign up."

"Well maybe I'll do that," he said. Sounded like he might have meant it, but he was still kind of tranced by the surroundings.

"My favorite word is *nincompoop*," Skitz called up from the water's edge. Even for Skitz this was a little off-the-topic, but Father was unfazed.

"Mine is *succulence*," Father answered, with authority, from his pulpit.

"Right, I'm signing up for your church too," Skitz announced.

It may be strange to say, but Skitz was sounding strange to me. He was approximately as daffy as usual, but there was a something in his voice—a hitch, a drag, something—that was unfamiliar. Maybe it was just the presence of a priest.

"*Nincompoop* is kind of an archaic word," Father said. "Where'd you hear it?"

"A nun called me that one time. And of course it made me laugh out loud. Which didn't make me less nincompoopy in her eyes, really."

"I wouldn't imagine it did," Father said. "But you were right to laugh. Always laugh at absurd things, Skitz, because if you can't do that, that's when you go crazy."

"I am crazy. You'd have to be nuts not to notice."

"He is," I said.

"He is not," Father insisted. "Listen, the only few occasions when I ever truly questioned my sanity was when I could not locate my sense of humor. If you can locate your sense of humor, then you are fine. Can you always locate your sense of humor?"

"Oh, I'm funny all the time," Skitz said, in a deeply serious tone.

"There you go, then," Father said. "I hereby pronounce you sane. And I'm a Jesuit, you know, so I can do that sort of thing."

"Wow," Skitz said, well impressed.

Sniff. There it was, or at least there part of it was. Skitz was sniffling a lot. Like crying or feeling pain, sniffling was something Skitz famously never, ever did. Despite his casual refusal to notice the extremes of New England weather, he never showed any symptoms of cold or flu or any other illness. He had the constitution of a buffalo.

"Are you sick?" I called down to him.

"Who, me?" he responded. "Of course not. Didn't you hear Father just then?"

"I don't mean mentally sick, I mean, do you have a cold or something?"

"No, shuddup."

"Fine, I'll shuddup, but I think maybe you're sick."

"That's not shuddup, Drew."

So I shuddup. It was peaceful there for a while, Skitz hugging the shore, Father hugging the Pulpit Elm.

Hector not saying a word, because Hector was not there. Hector should have been there.

"What is Father Shenanigan doing at Hector's?" I blurted, Skitz-like, so I must have been pretty bothered.

Father paused for a very long time.

"What is—" I tried.

"I wouldn't know," Father said, with less authority than he said most things. "He's helping the family," he added, unhelpfully.

"I don't know how much help he is," I said.

Father paused again. Then he said, "I'm still very much an outsider here. I don't know all that goes on. I have enough difficulty keeping myself out of trouble without monitoring the other residents of the rectory. I like it here. For once I'd like to stay put long enough to accomplish something."

"So why do you move so much?" I asked, like I asked before.

He paused again, twice as long. "I had a dog, too. His name was Frederick, half chow chow, half Irish setter. Red hair, black tongue, mad as a bee's nest. They wouldn't let me take him here. They wouldn't have Frederick here. It's been kind of hard for me without him," he said; then, "Been kind of hard . . ."

In the inevitable silence that slid in there I was left to

think whether he had answered my question. I think in some parallel-universe, Father Mullarkey way he had, at least partially. In a practical, understandable way, it was more like gobbledegook.

"I'm sorry about Frederick, Father, but why do they keep transferring you?"

Father pinched his lips up and grabbed at his beard. He stared at me silently, and looked for all the world like he was going to try and pull an answer out of his beard. It was not coming.

Something else came instead. On the heels of the Frederick story, I heard Skitz start crying.

Skitz Fitzsimmons. For the first time in all the time I knew him. Something was horribly wrong here.

"Hey," I shouted, angry, like he had not only let me down by breaking down, but like he had assaulted me personally, had threatened peace and stability and the whole world order. There was a shocking lack of compassion in my voice, because there was none in my gut. I was angry at Skitz. "Get up here, now!" I shouted.

Slowly, he did make his way up. I got off the Pulpit Elm steps, and Father came briskly down. We all got to roughly the same spot at roughly the same time, and I grabbed Skitz by the shoulders. Roughly.

"What is wrong with you?" I shook him, hard, and a lot. I wanted the pieces—nutty pieces that they were—to fall back together in the arrangement that I knew, not this.

Skitz did nothing, he said nothing. He just hung there, his bones rattling in my hands and his bizarre, misplaced tears rolling down his cheeks.

Until Father grabbed me. Carefully, he peeled my fingers from Skitz's shoulders, and eased me out of that full-on position. When he had himself in my place, directly in front of Skitz, he explained.

"I'm a very flawed Jesuit," he said gently, staring into Skitz's vacant eyes but seeming to speak to me. "But I do have my areas of expertise."

He continued to stare at Skitz, as if waiting for him to catch up and be ready for the next bit. "Have you been doing something you ought not to, Skitz?"

"That's all I ever do, isn't it?" Skitz muttered. "I'm garbage, Father. Just ask around."

Father held his ground. "You want to show me what you're up to?" he said.

Skitz nodded, slowly, and tears stopped. Father Mullarkey extended a great big open palm. Skitz fished around in his pocket, around and around and around as if it were a hay barn he was searching. Finally he came up with it. A very large tube of Krazy Glue.

"And what do you do with that?"

"Everything. It's Krazy Glue, Father. It can do everything."

"Yes, but what does it do for *this*?" He tapped Skitz on the forehead hard enough to jar it like a speed bag.

"Well," Skitz drawled, "when I breathe it in . . . I swim. I swim, and I float. And mostly, I just slow down and things go quiet. And I like it."

Father shook his shaggy head from side to side about ten times until Skitz involuntarily joined him. "You know what else you do?" Father said. "You kill your brain. You kill it, son. It'll be gone before you know it."

Skitz shrugged. "Nobody's gonna miss it, Father."

Father shook his head again, and looked like he was the one who would cry. But he didn't. He extended a big bear claw toward Skitz, and took the tube off him. "I'd miss it," he said. "I'd miss it something awful."

Skitz fell forward, crashing down safely in Father Mullarkey's grizzly embrace.

Which was good, because if Father let him go right now I was going to punch the boy dead.

FREAKS
SEEK FREAKS

NOT THAT ANYBODY ASKED ME, BUT MY FAVORITE WORD is neither *succulence* nor *nincompoop*—fine as they are—but *befriend*. Just the fact that it's there, that there is an actual verb-form word that describes the act of making yourself be a friend to somebody, makes me feel better about existence.

I didn't see either one of them for a few days, Skitz or Hector. They were both out of school. Nobody came to the windows at night. On Saturday I was so worked up I even wrapped up my paper route early and ducked into the six-forty-five A.M. Mass to see if one of them was serving.

It hadn't started yet, and I walked in through the

back entrance, in through the sacristy, where the priest and altar boys would be setting up shop.

"Well, this is a useful surprise," Father said. "Glad you could make it."

It was Monsignor Blarney, and if his words sounded like he was glad to see me, his big red face said what his big red face always said: *"Grrr."*

"Sorry, Monsignor, I was just looking to see if one of my friends was here serving this morning."

He was pulling his green Advent vestments over his head, and when he emerged, his mad white hair was all over the place, like a still photo of a blizzard.

"Well, as it happens, one of your friends was supposed to be here serving this morning. But he hasn't turned up."

"Oh, sorry, I'll just get out of—"

"So you're drafted. Go get into that cassock and surplice lying on that chair."

"What? Oh, except I'm not even supposed to be here, Monsignor. I just—"

"What has that got to do with anything? I'm not supposed to be here either. But when your housekeeper wakes you up with the news that you're the only priest in the house, then that's duty calling. And when your Monsignor tells you you are needed to serve at that same Mass, then that's duty calling."

His perma-grouch tone didn't leave a lot of room for debate, but I felt this was worth the risk.

"But I'm not an altar boy, you see."

"For heaven's sake, boy, have you not been to Mass several hundred times in your young life?"

"Yes, I have, sir, of course."

"Well, have you not been paying attention?"

Certainly, here was a situation with *no-win* scribbled all over it.

"I've been paying very close attention, Monsignor."

"Good. Then you know all there is to know. I'm asking you to serve at my Mass, not disable a nuclear device. If your friend Fitzsimmons can do it . . . Just suit up, and when I need you to do something during the service, I'll prompt you."

I'm sure you will, I thought. I couldn't believe it as I slipped into the two pieces of costume, the black dress-thing under the white dress-thing that made me look more like a nun than anything. After I had resisted every attempt to bring me into the team for so long, now here I was, just stumbling right into it. I felt like General Patton, waving his pearl-handled pistols at everybody through the whole of World War II, only to croak in a stupid car accident right after the shooting stopped. A guy just can't let his guard down, ever.

There was little fanfare at the six-forty-five compared to the big-game-day Masses of Sunday. There was no organ blaring us up onstage, and there were, maximum, twenty people scattered throughout a church that could hold probably two thousand. But still you had the feeling that these were the serious church athletes who wouldn't be happy with second-rate service. With me, they'd probably boo and throw things.

I kept it as simple as possible. I was more a follower than a leader, to be honest. I took my place off to the side of the altar, and kept my profile as low as I could get it. When the congregation stood, I stood. When they knelt or sat, I did the same. There was this small rack of bells placed on the carpet next to where I knelt, and I was vaguely aware of a couple of times during the service when they were supposed to be rung, but the harder I worked it out, the more elusive the details became. The only information that came clearly to mind was, as usual, the least helpful, when Skitz had told me that he just rang them whenever he felt happy.

The couple of times my hand reached near the bells, Monsignor looked my way and shook his head no.

So instead I acted primarily as a hanger-on, a well-behaved young nobody. I brought up the chalice when Father gestured toward it, and when it came time to deliver the actual Communion I went up, stood beside him, and held the plate under each chin. I felt very nervous, very much on show, very much like I shouldn't have been there, so it was better for me to have a little something to occupy me. But the way the Host was made—they said it was bread, but it seemed more like a big round paint chip—made it impossible to drop a crumb from it unless you chewed it and whistled and told a story at the same time. So again my job was pretty much ceremonial, and I spent the time reflecting the brass plate up off the underside of people's chins like you did with buttercups, to tell which ones liked butter. They all did.

I relaxed slightly when we had finished Communion, Monsignor was up there wiping up the silverware, and

I was off to the side again. There was not much left but for the priest to do a little wrap-up and then for us to march off in style, after which I could resume being me.

Except, first was the wild card.

Monsignor still had his back to the congregation, putting away the chalice in its ornamental cupboard at the feet of the giant wooden Christ-on-the-Cross that dominated from the back of the altar. One of the big doors at the far end of the church creaked open, letting in one last, seriously late Catholic. He took a seat in the very back row, but even from where I was, half a football field away, I could make out the hulking, hairy, denim-swathed figure.

Monsignor took no notice as far as I could see. He would have been used to all manner of lateness by now, and I was sure that you had to be a student at the school for him to mortifyingly announce in front of everybody that this Mass would not actually count for you, and you would have to come again later.

I wasn't listening to Monsignor's closing words as I fixated on Father Mullarkey down there at the back. I was up at the altar. He was in the back pew.

We had a seriously flip-flopped universe here, and I

was seriously looking forward to having it right side up again.

Next thing I knew, Monsignor, who had finished the words bit and had circled around to the front of the altar in preparation for departure, was glaring at me and stamping one foot like a Clydesdale.

I scrambled, took my place next to him, bowed with him to giant Jesus, and we made our exit.

"You weren't kidding about not being qualified," Monsignor said as he pulled his robe back up over his head, stirring up the snowstorm again.

"Sorry, Monsignor," I said, getting disrobed just as quickly. I hung the cassock and surplice on a hook next to a series of similar getups, and scooped up my newspaper bag. I stood there, waiting to be dismissed.

He continued about his business, hanging his gear on hangers and placing them in a closet next to lots of other Mardi Gras–colored fancy dress. He got a look at himself in the closet-door mirror and flattened down his hair, a little. Then he caught me in his field of view.

"You don't get paid, if that's what you're thinking," he said.

I wanted to say, You're welcome, but I didn't quite have the guts. One of the rare occasions I wished I were Skitz. "I'll just go, then," I said.

"You just will," he said, and pushed his hair down for the mirror again.

I went out of the sacristy, back out along the side of the altar, and into the main body of the church building. All of the people from the Mass had left now, except for the last one, who was still catching up.

"Hi," I said when I finally made it all the way back to him.

"Hi," he said, smiling unsurely.

"You saw my debut," I said.

"Just about."

"I shouldn't have been up there."

He inhaled really deeply, like he was gonna huff and puff and blow the house down. "I should have," he said, and exhaled all that air.

Ouch. You could hardly call it air. It was not a pleasant breeze, and it was a stink I was familiar with. Smelled like my dad. Or at least like the parts of the house he has frequented, like the sour end of the couch, the front hallway carpet, and every corner of the bathroom. And it wasn't just Father's breath. It was coming off of him all over.

"This was supposed to be your Mass?" I asked.

He nodded.

"What did you do?"

He frowned with mock concentration. At least it looked like mock. Could even have been mock-mock concentration.

"Well, I was out. And about. Those are my two favorite places, out and about. I go there whenever I can."

"Right," I said blankly. "What does a person do in these places?"

"Mostly drink. See, Drew, I like the odd drink."

"If you don't mind my saying so, Father, I think you like the even ones too."

"Hah." He laughed and slapped his leg loud enough to reverb it around the church.

I looked quickly all around, worried we'd be seen, heard, smelled. I felt like Father's problems, like his odor, could somehow swamp me over, cling to me, glue us somehow together in wrongness. This was probably not the best place to be hanging out. "Are you just getting back now?" I asked him.

He looked at his watch, like that was going to help him answer. "I went down to the river on my way home—I hope you don't mind, I've been borrowing your Pulpit Elm. It is an ungodly beautiful thing. Makes you want to be there all the time."

"Don't mind at all, Father. But, do you think it was a good idea missing Mass?"

He shrugged. "Time gets away from you," he said. "At least it does from me. I'll see loads of time in front of me and then before I know it minutes come to hours, and hours come to nothing."

Father looked down at his feet, then up at me with a weak smile. We hit a small silent patch then, which I knew wouldn't hold for long.

"I'm going to be in some trouble, I suspect," he said.

I couldn't quite imagine the conditions for a priest being in trouble. Especially a giant priest, a giant Jesuit.

"I don't know. It'll probably be fine," I said with all my authority. I had just served Mass, after all.

Apparently Father thought there was something to that. "You think?" he said, paused, answered, "It will be fine. You're right. Things will always be fine, if you have faith. I've been running on faith for a good long time now."

That was a bit of a puzzler, that one, because he looked at me like I was supposed to respond somehow. The only thing I was thinking was that he was suddenly sounding a little old-style and priestly to me and neither one of us would think that was good. So I didn't say it.

So he straightened me out.

"As long as you have faith. What you have faith *in*, that's your own business. Would you like to hear those records now? You still haven't had a chance to hear my records."

He stood up as if I had already answered. He let his big stinky face open up in the hairiest child-smile imaginable at the thought of finally sharing his records.

I didn't want to hear the records.

And I didn't want to tell him no.

"Sure," I said, and before I could even think about where we might be going, we were there.

At the back of the schoolyard, the spot where the school buildings and the convent and the church and the rectory were equidistant away, were the garages.

You never thought about them too much because they were just there, a four-berth red brick box that worked as a surface for off-the-wall, or a street hockey goal when we chalked it up. But the priests' cars were too big and the nuns only seemed to pull out their one car when nobody was looking, so it became for most people just one more chunk of the solid immovable timeless Blessed Sacrament scenery with nothing going on inside.

That was incorrect.

Apparently as a concession to, or a protest against, Father Mullarkey's particular taste and style, he was allotted a kind of cultural outhouse, taking up one whole empty bay of the garage.

He led me around the side, bypassing the big monster wooden doors that took at least two nuns and whoever they could grab on the odd occasion they needed it opened. It looked like raising the flag on Iwo Jima, when we'd all help out. There he got out his keys and let us in the normal, person-size door.

And led me down, past the resident Chrysler, white with a fake leather black roof, to the far end of the garage, where he flipped a switch and enlightened all.

One single, strong, yellow-orange bulb hanging from a ceiling fixture washed the place with a warm sort of haze. Father walked to a freestanding unit near the wall and turned it on, and right away an electric space heater buzzed to life.

It was a clubhouse. Like a very fun, very hippie den that maybe an eighteen-year-old would have in the basement if his parents were demented enough to let him. There was an overstuffed sofa that looked like it was made from perfectly broken-in cowhide catcher's mitts, and a plaid tub chair made from that Herculon stuff that heals itself after you stab it with a pen. There was a very big stereo stacked in the corner, set on top of a table that was actually a big wooden spool that public utility companies coil wire on, turned on its side. There was another spool in the middle of the floor, covered in books and albums. There were three posters up on the wall. One of Jimi Hendrix kneeling in front of his guitar on fire, underneath script that said "I'm the one who has to die, when it's time for me to die. So let me live my life the way I want to." Another was a painted profile of Bob Dylan with rainbows for hair, and what looked like Mount Washington where his nose should have been. The third showed a body on a hospital gurney with a sheet covering it like he was dead, with a guitar frozen in his hand. It read JOHN ENTWISTLE'S RIGOR MORTIS.

My face must have showed how far away I was from knowing what that meant, because Father pointed at it, saying with a nod, "John Entwistle. The Ox. Played bass for The Who."

He smiled knowingly. I doubt my expression changed at all.

But that didn't mean I wasn't impressed.

"This is amazing," I said, walking around, checking it out. "A person could live in here, if it had a fridge and a toilet and a little more heat."

He was clearly proud to be showing it off. I didn't imagine he had a lot of opportunities.

"Ya," he said, walking to the stereo and flipping through a standing row of albums on the floor three feet deep. "It's no Pulpit Elm, but it has got tunes. Who knows, if I play my music loud enough maybe my roommates will give me a whole other house for myself."

"Worth a shot," I said.

I sat down in the tub chair, and I had to say, it also had a stale and familiar whiff to it. Like Father now, and more.

He put on a record, waited for it to produce sound as he hovered down there on his haunches. When it did it came up as a sort of rolling military drum march with matching bass for an introduction, followed by some electric guitar squalling. "Yes," Father said, and turned the music up uncommonly loud for a Saturday morning that hadn't seen eight o'clock yet. The heater was blowing pretty good beside me now, which was good for the bones, though less so for the nose.

Father sat down across from me, across the spool.

"Jefferson Airplane," he said, closing his eyes and nodding to the military beat and the surely not military lyrics. *One pill makes you larger, and one pill makes you small / And the ones that mother gives you, don't do anything at all . . .*

Father didn't open his eyes again until the whole song had played out, rising up really high from its slow-rumble beginning until by the end it was kind of a shout. Again, for the time of day.

Father opened his eyes with this very pleased, satisfied look, like he had just finished an excellent meal.

"I wanted to show you here," he said warmly, "after you showed me your tree. Isn't it nice?"

It was nice. "It is," I said.

He smiled for a couple more seconds, then he reached across, across the divide, over the spool table, and he slapped his great hand down on my knee. He slapped it again, then gave it a squeeze, just above my knee.

"You know, you're the best friend I have made here, Drew. Since I've been here. My very best friend."

I had I think a smile frozen onto my face as I looked right at Father and he looked right at me. I felt my whole head rush with an overflow of blood, and I got really hot, and I couldn't even tell you fully why. I didn't think it was wrong, but I didn't feel right; I didn't feel threatened, but I didn't quite feel safe; I didn't feel angry at all, but I didn't feel happy either. I didn't like Father one bit less, but I wanted to give him back his hand.

So I did, without hesitation.

"Sorry," Father said, taking the one hand with the other, as if these were actually two different beings

I was dealing with. Then he wrung them together. "Sorry, Andrew, I didn't mean anything wrong."

"Fine," I said. "It's okay. I'm just like that. Don't like people putting hands on me, you know."

"I know," he said, and hopped up as the next song kicked up louder than the last one. He kept his back to me as he fussed at the stereo.

Another thing I never got about people and their music, especially rock people. Why, when a song came on that was louder than the previous one, did they get all excited and turn the volume up *louder*? Hasn't the record itself already done that?

"Do you think that's a good idea?" I asked as Father came back from tweaking the fat volume button.

He nodded. "Nobody ever bothers me out here. That's one of the things that make it such a special place. Nobody ever bothers me here."

I nodded, smiled, tried to enjoy the music. But I wasn't enjoying it. It was making me uneasy. Maybe if it were quieter. I was uneasy anyway. Father was enjoying it, or trying hard to, leaning back in his sofa, smiling at the ceiling. I was uneasy.

"Andrew," he said, and he had to say it loudly over

the music. "Are you cool?"

I wasn't entirely sure what I had heard, loud as it was. "What?"

"I asked you if you were cool. Are you, cool?"

He was going to start to think the puzzled face was my natural face because I could feel it, with us again.

"I . . . guess," I said.

He sat up, leaned forward and pulled a shortbread-cookie tin out from under his sofa. He opened it and pulled out cigarette papers, and started shaking up the rest of the contents of the tin like he was panning for gold.

"Oh," I said. "Oh. Cool. Well, sorry, when I said cool . . . There are different kinds of cool, aren't there. . . ."

I thought this must have been the uncoolest-ever response to the cool question because a look of mortal horror struck Father Mullarky's great, robust face. He also looked, I suddenly noticed, really young behind that bushy beard.

He was looking, actually, beyond me.

A firm hand clamped down on my shoulder, and I gasped. Then I looked up over me, into the flaming face of Monsignor Blarney, and I gasped a whole second time.

"Turn off that damn music," Monsignor said to Father, who sat there paralyzed.

"Go home, son," Monsignor said to me, and I would not have scrambled out of there faster if it was the Grim Reaper himself with his claw on my shoulder.

———

TRIBE

RUNNING ON FAITH. AS LONG AS YOU HAD FAITH YOU'D always be fine. What you had faith *in*, however, was your own business.

Right. I took my sponge ball and I stomped my way to Skitz's house. No more letting stuff happen or not happen, I was going to make it happen.

I threw my ball against his steps. And I threw and threw. His front porch was all wood, as were the steps, and truth was, they should have been replaced or at least extensively repaired a long time ago. That was bad if you were walking up there, over dry and creaking, cracking boards, but good if you were throwing a ball against them with the aim of making a persistent hollow thwacking racket.

Which I was. I threw and threw and threw until my arm started to ache because the ball was getting cold and heavy and wet from picking up the remains of a light snow that was now converting to a bit of mush on the ground. So I switched to my left hand, which I like to do sometimes, awkward as it is, and I threw and threw some more. This would drive Skitz's mother nuts, but she wouldn't come out. She never came out, not even to the window.

Finally, when the ball weighed about five pounds and was making a sound like a wrecking ball pummeling a building, Skitz made his appearance.

"My ma says shuddup, wouldja." He stood in his doorway, as if he was going to disappear right back in there again.

"I know she does," I said, and thumped the ball off the steps again.

"Quit it, Drew," he said.

"C'mon out." I said. "We can play some Boston–New York off your steps."

He thought it was a question. "Nah," he said.

Thump, my sponge ball said. It was a great throw,

really, right off the top edge of the second-top step, so it caromed up, ricocheted off the porch ceiling, the wall, the porch, then bumbled back down to me after it had made a glorious racket.

"*Bwaaah,*" Mrs. Skitz squalled from far off in there somewhere.

"All right, all right," he said. "I'm coming out." He shut the door behind him.

"Get a coat or something, wouldja, numbskull," I said.

"Fine," he said, moping back inside for his skimpy thin jacket.

I waited right there at the foot of his stairs until he had descended and was right in front of my face. I stared at him, at his skin, at his mouth, but mostly at his eyes, to see what I could see. I had somehow taken my eyes off him in the recent past and let something important get past me, and that wasn't going to happen anymore. The eyes told the story. Dry, clear, nervous. Googly, but dry. Bright as new pennies, and spinning like whirligigs. As they should have been. My boy was back.

"You okay?" I asked.

"Ya, I'm okay," he said, kind of touchy. He looked away. I craned around, to follow his face with my face and bring him back.

"'Cause I'll kill ya," I assured him, once I had him back.

"Well, duh," he said. "Don't you think I know that? What do you think I been hiding from?"

I took a few steps backward, thought about it, and decided to smile. "So you do have a little bit of sense in you somewhere."

"Don't get carried away," he said, and grabbed the ball out of my hand as I raised it to bounce off his mother's steps.

"Good to have you back," I said. "Now let's go retrieve the other one."

"There's another one?" he asked seriously.

On the way to Hector's house, I told Skitz the tale of my adventure at the Mullarkey Lounge.

He was dumbfounded. "*You* served at Mass?" he asked, getting right to the meat of the issue, as usual.

"This is serious, Skitz," I said. "I think there could

be some real trouble."

"So you're an altar boy now. You are finally on the team. How was it? Did you ring the bells? Don't you love the bells?"

"Shuddup, wouldja. Didn't you hear any of the rest of what I said?"

"Of course I did. The lounge sounds amazing. Can we go there? Maybe he'll let us use it sometimes. This could be so cool, we could have parties and stuff. Is there a TV?"

I sighed. "There is no TV, and I seriously doubt there is a Mullarkey Lounge by now, judging from the look of Monsignor's big fat red head last time I saw him."

"Oh," Skitz said, quieter now, solemn. "Then I missed it completely. Why does everything happen to me?"

I had to stop right there in the street, to turn and look at his stupid face to see if he was joking.

His stupid face said he was not, in fact, joking to begin with. But because Skitz's mouth is so often so much faster than his brain, it can sometimes take him longer to digest his own words than it takes others to digest them. I stared at him and waited for the gap to close.

He grinned, laughed, shook his head. "Shuddup, Skitz, wouldja," he said. His grin gave me a good view of his Krazy Glued tooth.

"You ever gonna get that fixed the right way?" I asked, pointing.

"What?" he said, sounding just slightly offended. "Why? No. Why?"

When finally we got to Hector's, I skipped the usual and the unusual approaches to reaching him. His window had proven useless, and you could not Boston–New York him out like you could with Skitz. And even though I had not been inside the house before, they didn't mind you ringing the bell.

We rang three times before giving up. We peeped a little bit, where we could, through lace curtains and shades with small gaps. We walked down the alley, around the back, and up again to the street side. There didn't appear to be any sign of life anywhere.

"So, what do we do now?" Skitz asked.

I stared up at the house, up and down the street, back at the house again.

"Boston–New York?" I said.

"I'll give you a game," he said, took the ball and walked up close to Hector's steps. He bounced one sharply off the edge of the bottom step, which went high in the air and made me back up almost to the opposite-side curb before I caught it.

"That's one out, boy," I said and threw the ball back.

He gave me a game, then another, then another. Then we switched to stickless street hockey, kicking the ball with our feet and using Hector's steps as a goal. Then we sat on the steps for a while and ate a bag of sunflower seeds until we got cold. Then we played Boston–New York.

Eventually we quit. Eventually the day ended, the darkness came and the serious cold came and the Fossas family did not. Eventually we went home.

That night, though late in the night, though deep in the sleep it took me so long to reach, I greeted the sound of the tapping at my window like an old friend. Like it was Santa Claus a week early and a couple of years late, rather than a nuisance.

I was quick to the shade, and looked down with anticipation.

Until, then, I had to look up.

"Father?" I said.

"Could you come out?" he asked.

"I guess I could."

We started walking without talking as soon as I reached the lawn. There was little doubt where we would be headed, anyway.

He didn't smell quite like the last time. Maybe a little. But he was unsteady, in some invisible way. The bear was gone, that was for sure, and something more wary was in its place.

"I'm packed," he said as we approached the tree. "I'm history here."

"You're leaving? Already?"

He nodded. He mounted the steps of the Pulpit Elm with some relish, absorbing the sound of the creaking he created in a similar way to how he absorbed music.

"Transferred," he said. "I wasn't ever going to be a good fit with this group, so it was just a matter of time. I thought it would be a matter of *more* time, but what can you do?"

I had seen priests come and go before. Monsignor was here before running water, and Shenanigan had been there long enough to have dropped some unchoppable roots, but that third spot in the big house seemed to be a basically permanent third-wheel situation. They came and they went, and some were decent guys and some were less decent guys, but you know, I didn't care much. It was all about the same to me.

This was not the same to me.

"Kinda sucks, Father," I said, and walked around the tree, down to the water where Skitz would usually be. From there I could look up, and through the darkness make out the side view of Father looking out over his congregation.

"Kind of does suck, Andrew," he said. "But life moves on, it always does, and we're not here to fret about me."

"We're not."

"We're not. You are a good friend, Andrew. You were my friend while I was here. More importantly, you are a good friend to people who really need you, people who probably can't do without you. I'm here to urge you, before I go, to continue to be a good friend. No matter what anybody tells you."

I stood there now, looking up at him, listening to him the way I often saw folks, really religious folks, looking up when one of the priests in the church would mount the curlicue stairs to rant at them. I thought those people all looked stupid.

"Who's going to tell me what?"

"You've got a good little tribe there, Andrew. And all of life winds up being driven by tribes. Your family, your school, your profession, your denomination. Your friends. Your tribe is quality. I wish I could join your tribe."

"You can. You have."

"Thanks. But I can only ever be an honorary member, which I will remain honored to be for the rest of my life. Closer to home, though, stick tight with the tribe you have. Look out for one another. If you ever can't count on your tribe, on the people who are supposed to be there for you—if they, in fact, turn out to be your problem—then you are well and truly wasted, my young friend."

If church really was any good, I thought, it would be more like this. A little warmer, maybe, but more like this. I could watch him, and listen to him, even if at the same time he was making me sadder than I wanted to be and I was not sure why.

"Okay," I said. I picked up a rock and plunked it in the water.

"I love that sound, when I can't see the water," he said.

I always loved that sound, when I couldn't see the water.

"My tribe is kind of shrunk at the moment, Father."

"Yes. I know."

"Do you know what the story is?"

"Yes. I do. Hector is sick, Drew. He's in St. Elizabeth's."

"What?" I shouted. I turned back up to him in the Pulpit, but he was gone. I stood there listening to him creak step after step of the ancient thing as he came down. Then he walked around the tree to the riverside. "What?" I snapped again.

"Not sure exactly." He put his hands on my shoulders. I slapped them away. "He had been dizzy, sweating, complaining of headaches and ringing in his ears. Then he fainted, and they took him in. He's got bleeding, in his stomach, apparently."

I marched right past him and started stomping away. He caught up to me and grabbed me from behind. I tried again to shake him off, but that was when I found how strong a bear can be.

He held me tight, close to him, from behind until I stopped struggling. I felt him breathing in my ear.

We stayed like that for maybe a whole minute. Maybe more, even. I felt his head lean more heavily on mine, felt his breathing, even and warm, thick over me. "I told you," I said, "I don't like this. I don't like people putting their hands on me."

He didn't let go. "There is obviously nothing for you to do right now, except go home. He's not going to die or anything. He's going to get better. But he needs you to be his friend, all the time."

"You're a good friend," Father said again, then shoved me away. "Remain a good friend no matter what they say to you."

He was stalking off now, faster than I had ever seen him move before, away from me and away from here. Light snow was starting to come down again. "What's wrong with Hector?" I said, walking after him, but not fast enough to catch up.

"I don't know, Andrew," he said. "I have to go. I was not supposed to even do this much. I am out of chances. If they find out I even had contact with you, I'm finished. It's bad enough. I have my own troubles. Good-bye, Andrew, it has been a pleasure knowing you. Pray for me."

I stopped following him, not that I was keeping up with his yard-long strides anyway.

"I don't pray," I said. "I beg."

"That'll do fine," he called back.

Suddenly, as I watched him tromp across the baseball fields getting dusty with snow, I felt a rush of anger. He looked like he was running away, from me personally, from everything he was supposed to change and improve. He was leaving a big whopping hole, a hole that wasn't even there till he came and dug it.

"Not good enough!" I screamed.

"Maybe not," he called back. "I'm sorry."

"No!" I shouted again, and when he didn't stop, I ran.

I ran across the field and caught up to him and when I did I threw myself at him with both hands and shoved him as hard as I could from behind.

It barely budged him, but it did get him to turn around. When he did, he had a bottle in his hand that he must have had in his coat—whiskey, half drunk. He stared straight at me, then tipped way back for a long drink that made me queasy just to see it. His eyes watered when he brought the bottle down and capped it. He slid it back in the inside pocket.

"You wanted to say something?" he said.

"You don't have to leave like that," I said. "They don't just shove you out the door the same day they tell you. I've seen these guys come and go before, and it doesn't work like that. You have time. You've been transferred hundreds of times, so you know, you have time. What's the rush?"

An angry scowl flashed over his face, and I took a step back. Not that it was so horrifying, but it was so *strange*. But it was gone again as quickly.

"I am scheduled to leave Monday night. Until then I am basically under house arrest in the rectory. But that's beside the point because the point is I want to go," he said. "Now. Good-bye, Drew, and good luck." He turned again and walked.

I tracked him.

"Maybe we could use your help, before you leave."

"You don't need me."

"Maybe we do."

"No, you don't."

"Maybe you're just a coward. Maybe you shouldn't have gotten people's hopes up and pretended you were different."

"Maybe I am. Maybe I shouldn't."

He was frustrating me now to the point of madness. "Or maybe you're just running away because you want to do to me what Shenanigan is doing to Hector. Maybe that's why you have trouble keeping your damn hands to your damn self. Is that it? Huh? Father Friendly? Is that it?"

He sure turned now. He spun and ran back in my direction like a linebacker. I wanted to be tough, I wanted to provoke him, and I wanted to be cool, but when I saw it for real, I wanted to run. I started backpedaling.

But like most linebackers, he was a lot faster than he looked. He caught me, grabbed me with one powerful hand, held me by the upper arm, and gave me a fierce whack with the other, right across my face. He drew back to do it again, and I found myself watching in terror, focused on the hand as it went away, went high, then came whistling toward me again. It was a fist when it peaked. Then it unfolded slowly, in stop time, in midair, as it came to me, came to me, opened up, and the open hand splashed across the side of my face, catching the whole side of my face.

"How dare you," he said, panting, red as raw beef. "I was good to you. I was too good to you and I got ruined for that. Do you know . . . Do you know how dangerous that kind of talk could be for me? Do you realize what you could be doing to me?"

I could not feel any pain on my face because I could not feel anything, physically. I was hung on the words that had come out of me.

They were horrible. How could I say them? They were the worst words, and the only thing for sure was that I had said them, and that because of them either Father was awful, or I was. It couldn't be both.

But right now, it didn't even matter. We didn't matter.

"Don't tell me about how bad it is for *you*, Father, huh? Tell me something that matters. Father Shenanigan is doing it to Hector, isn't he?"

He was staring very oddly at the side of my face, which must have been pretty welted. "I'm sorry," he said, reaching an open hand to touch the spot.

"Shuddup," I said, yanking away. "I don't care about this. Answer me. Father Shenanigan is doing it to Hector, isn't he?"

It was as if he were lost, in himself, in what he had done to me, in whatever problems he had that had gotten him to this place and had gotten him shoved back out again. He looked obsessively at the marks on my face. "I did not mean to hurt you."

"Father!" I snapped. "Isn't he?"

He stopped, but he held the faraway look.

His mouth opened, I saw his lips move just slightly, his tongue appear just a peek and then withdraw again, like a dying man trying, and failing, to get out last words.

Then he pulled his bottle out. He uncapped it, tipped it all the way back, and drank it all the way empty.

He let the bottle drop out of his hand onto the snowy ground, and stared glassy-eyed at me. He was the biggest mess I had ever laid eyes on.

"I'm sorry," he said.

Every muscle in my body tensed to stone. All my blood shot to my face like a giant was squeezing me out of a tube.

"Don't say *sorry*!" I screamed. "Say *no*. I am not asking you to be sorry. I don't even care if you are sorry. I am asking you a question and you need to tell me the answer and the answer is no, so say *no*! Say it, now. Say *no*!"

He did not understand. He did not get it. What the hell was wrong with this creature in front of me, because, after all that, what he said was "I'm sorry," again.

I felt, suddenly, the sensation Skitz had described with the glue. I was swimming, I was floating. Rather, the ground below me and the city around me were liquifying, moving and flowing and blurring, and I couldn't imagine why anyone would feel like it was desirable. Not even Skitz.

Because the thing is, I had never really believed it. I

didn't think that was happening to Hector or to anybody else, no matter what I said, no matter what jokes I made, no matter what my feelings told me or the circumstances told me or my own good gut told me. I never, ever believed it, even up to the very second I asked Father Mullarkey about it and in spite of whatever in hell possessed me to ask him.

Even now. Even right up to now, I don't believe it. I don't doubt it's true. But I don't believe it.

Father Mullarkey believed it, though. Knew about it. Lived with it. Kept it within the Franchise.

My head was so muzzy I hardly even noticed Father Mullarkey slither away.

"Hey, *best friend*?" I called. "Go to hell, *best friend*, okay? Thanks for everything, *shepherd*. Take care of yourself, *best friend*." He was almost out of earshot, but he was not out of earshot. "*Vaya con Dios, Padre*, and don't come back, okay?"

He answered in that almost supernatural low-hum rumble I got to know in the beginning, but it carried back all the way across the fields as clearly as if he were sitting across the Papa Gino's table from me.

He said something, but it was nothing.

IF I EVER FALL BEHIND

WHEN WE CAME INTO SCHOOL ON MONDAY WE WERE starting the last short week before the Christmas vacation, and it was about time. We would be out Wednesday at lunch and would do hardly any real work in the meantime, so these would be the peak of the Christmas Spirit days. Tuesday we would deliver meals to the old folks in the Heath Street projects, Wednesday we would clean the whole school and then watch *It's a Wonderful Life* and then talk about its deeper spiritual resonance and then be gone. Really though, it had been some years since I'd last gotten the full boot out of the holiday, though I still liked it fine. I could be reasonably sure of getting things I wanted for Christmas because being a sports guy made things simple for folks, present-wise. A new hockey stick, maybe an Oakland A's or Minnesota Vikings jersey. There were more Bruins books every year explaining either why they weren't winning Stanley Cups or why it was finally their time again, so there was certain to be one I hadn't read yet. But at school they could tape up all the cutout angels they wanted, they could build a papier-mâché manger scene so lifelike you'd swear the little haloed baby was going to start squawking any minute, they could get us to sing "God Rest Ye Merry, Gentlemen" until we were so merry we might fall over, but none of that was going to make it what it used to be. That was gone. I knew it already two years ago, but I knew it to death this year.

It was just a vacation now. Not Christmas, not really.

And as if to drive the point home, the white-haired, red-faced nightmare that greeted us first thing was definitely not Santa.

"You may by now have been hearing rumors," Monsignor intoned. "Or perhaps not, but at any rate I would like to address any playground talk that might be had. First, regarding Hector Fossas. He is in St. Elizabeth's Hospital, and I'm afraid won't be out before the end of term this week. It was hoped that he might be able to come out for the class Christmas party today, but I don't think it will happen. Now, he is going to be fine—he has a stomach ailment, but it is being treated—and he will be back with you good as new for the start of classes after the new year. Sister tells me you will be making cards, both Christmas *and* get-well"— he must have considered that humor, because he paused and bared his teeth in a way I had never seen before— "to decorate and sign and send along to him.

"Secondly, Father Mullarkey, after having experienced a series of difficulties settling into life here at Blessed Sacrament, and after some questions regarding his role here, will be going away for a period of convalescence and a spiritual retreat. After this time it was agreed that he would be transferred to another parish, where he will be able to get a fresh start. We wish Father Mullarkey all the best, we thank him for all his good work, we hope to hear soon of his return to serving the people of the archdiocese as he has done so well hadn't happened at a Christmas service since we'd shown up at the place as drooly little six-year-olds.

When I got back to the class, Skitz was sitting alone at his desk eating his lunch. He had his brown bag torn open and spread across his desk like a tablecloth, like he does. He looked like they beat him up, the way they know how without leaving marks.

I went and got my lunch from off the windowsill where we keep them.

"She said I have one more chance. I'm on probation, Drew," Skitz said, his eyes darting all over the place, as if probation were some big beast that was stalking him. "They said they're getting serious now. They said I broke the window—"

"Which you did."

"Which I did. And they said I was in fights and I was drunk at the Bruins game and there is I guess a lot of wine missing from the sacristy storage closet. . . ."

"Which you did not do," I said, with a lot more hope than certainty.

"Which I did not do," he said, with enough sad certainty for both of us.

We each waited for the other to say something now

that would straighten it all out.

"Drew, man, they're kicking me out if I don't do everything right from now on. They'll send me to public school. They'll put me on the buses. I can't go on the buses. I can't go without you guys, you know that. You know that, and *they* know that. I'm just barely making it as it is, and now I have to be perfect. I'll never last out there. I need my friends."

"Calm down," I said. "We'll just have to make sure you're perfect from here on, that's all. No big deal."

I looked as solemn as I could, nodding at him. He did exactly the same, only he wasn't joking.

Then he caught on and we both broke out laughing.

"And you know what?" Skitz said.

"What?" I said.

"Sister says the only reason I'm even getting this chance is because Father Mullarkey came in and begged her."

"He. . . ?"

"Ya," Skitz said, going back to his earnest, persevering face. "So I owe him, don't I? I owe it to him, to be perfect."

I was trying to picture Father coming in and doing

that. In the middle of all whatever. It was a fuzzy picture, but it was there. In the middle of everything, after what I said. I was already feeling bad about it all. I was feeling guilty. Even after he punched me. Then this.

"You do," I said.

We all ate our lunches and got to gab a lot more than usual, and as lunch wound down it casually morphed into what passed for a party in our school. Various teachers' pets were called up one at a time to collect large economy-size bags of Christmas candies and come along row by row and distribute portions on our desks. Chunks of ribbon candy thin as paper, curvy and sticky. Mini–candy canes, three each. Big candy canes, one each. Snowman- and Santa-shaped gingerbread cookies, which clashed with The Message but were allowed because nobody made ginger Jesuses and it just showed how relaxed and cool we could be when we were in the mood. A Dixie cup full of Coke each, with refills. Caramel popcorn.

Sister wheeled out the stereo, and on came the same versions of the Christmas carols we always sang to.

It wasn't half bad. It wasn't a party you would actually ever *go* to, but for one that was dropped on you in school, it wasn't half bad. It seemed like people were trying. It seemed like people were okay.

Father Mullarkey begged for Skitz.

O come, all ye faithful, / Joyful and triumphant. . . .

There were a handful of diehards, all of them girls, who still gave out Christmas cards to everyone. Hector would have snuck one into my desk by now, if we had Hector. Sister gave the word, and they came around with their deliveries.

Skitz was overcome. He gets overcome every year. But this was different.

"I love it here, Drew. I really want to stay here."

We three kings of Orient are, / Bearing gifts we traverse afar. . . .

Suddenly Sister cut off the music. Looking at the shoe box window in the door at the front of the room, she announced, "I have a special surprise for you now."

The door opened, and in walked Hector Fossas, followed closely, like a boxer and his manager, by Father Shenanigan.

And it was as if he was a for-real boxing champion, the ovation he got. Everyone thundered, stomping feet, whistling and hooting until Sister finally shushed us.

It felt like I hadn't seen him since third grade. He waved at me, and at Skitz. We waved back. He looked extremely thin, and greenish, and he moved as if he were walking across a beach full of broken shells. He was wearing sweatpants, a sweatshirt, and sneakers, which here made him seem more foreign than anything.

"Now," Father announced, "Hector cannot stay long, but he really wanted to come out for this party. I have to have him back in an hour, so enjoy him while you can." With that, Hector took steps in our direction. "But no candy!" Father said, really loud. He must have thought that was how a joke was told.

"You may all get up and move around," Sister said, and then turned to pay too much respect to Father Shenanigan.

The music came back on.

Joy to the world, the Lord is come! / Let earth receive her King. . . .

We immediately tugged Hector to the back of the room, then over to the windows. Skitz hopped up and sat in the sill, and we all huddled as close as decently possible.

"You all right?" I asked hurriedly.

"I'm good," he said.

"Don't die," Skitz said.

"Okay," Hector said.

"How's your stomach?" I asked.

"Stomach's fine now. Lots better."

"Was it something you ate?" Skitz asked.

I saw three ships come sailing in on Christmas Day, on Christmas Day. . . .

"Ya, Skitz," Hector said, and peeled open a wide grin that made him look more skeletal, and made him look sadder than when he didn't smile.

"Do you think," I said seriously, "that maybe eating aspirin all the time might not be a good idea?"

He didn't say anything, but he nodded.

"Oh no," Skitz said. "Not St. Joe's."

"You still getting headaches?" I pressed.

"I'm all right."

"Is there anything else, Hec? Anything else wrong with ya?"

He pulled his lips really tight, so they looked like eighty-year-old lips. He looked like a toughened, leathery old solid, like there was no blood or fluid in him of any kind.

"I'm fine," he said.

"Really? 'Cause if there's something else . . . if there's anything else you want to tell us, man . . ."

He got really close to me then, right up close to my face. Then I felt him tug on my belt. He grabbed me by the belt, and he pulled up, he pulled really hard, and sick or not this was the strongest guy you ever wanted to meet.

"Remember I said if I ever fell behind. . . ?"

From his perch up on the sill, Skitz started kicking. He kicked me to let me know company was on the way.

"What are you doing?" Father asked in exaggerated shock. "Andrew, what are you doing here, getting Hector worked up? This boy is sick."

He's not the only one, Father, is what I was thinking.

I didn't say it. Miraculously, Skitz didn't say it either. We were learning.

Father told Hector it was time to go, even though it had been nothing like an hour, but I guess I spoiled everything. I guess I got too close to the patient and one of us might be poisoning the other from the contact. Father headed to the front. "Let's go," he said to Hector.

Hector lingered, my face inches from his gaunt face. "I'm falling behind, Drew," he said, giving my belt a last, painful tug. "I'm falling."

He followed when Father called him once more. Father stopped by the door and waved and wished us all a blessed Christmas and left just like that with our Hector like he had him on a rope. Hector's eyes were still on me as the door closed.

And they were still on me afterward.

The party got back to where it was, we got back to our seats, we ate candy and we listened to music but we didn't talk much and we didn't sing. I wasn't focused on a single thing for the rest of the afternoon except the sound of the school bell that was going to let us out of there.

"I've never even been to a hospital before," Skitz said, like we were on a field trip to an amusement park.

"Ya, well behave yourself or they'll keep you for observation."

St. Elizabeth's Hospital in Brighton was not along any of my usual travel routes, but I knew the way fine, just the way I knew the way to most of the stops on most of the routes, the green, orange, red, even blue lines of the MBTA. I studied the maps habitually as I rode, and thought a lot about opportunities that might come up to bring me to one of the places I never went to before. I wanted to be ready.

And I was. I got off on Washington Street and walked up the white rock stairs of the Catholic Church's big Boston medical facility. It looked expensive. I wondered who was going to pay for this, for Hector.

I worked out the hospital setup the same way I worked out the MBTA setup, and it was nearly as elaborate. But eventually I located where Hector was. Visiting hours were two to four, seven to nine. We were right on time for daytime visiting.

We hit the nurses' station on Hector's floor, and I asked for him. The nurse in charge held up a wait-a-minute finger, and made a call.

Practically by the time she had hung up the receiver and told us wait a minute, sweeties, he was there.

Father Shenanigan.

"What are you doing here, Andrew?" he asked.

"I'm here to see Hector."

"I'm here too," Skitz said, even though it was glaringly obvious. It just wasn't obviously obvious to Father Shenanigan.

"You're not expected. You really need to make arrangements before presuming you can just come marching in like this."

"Ya, but we came to see Hector."

"You saw him today already."

"Well, we like him," Skitz said, "so we thought we might like to see him again."

"You can't see him right now."

"But it's visiting hours. And he'll want to see us."

"Well, I'm sorry, but you can't."

He was really making me mad, making me careless with my manners, which I like to think are normally pretty good.

"Who are you? Why are you here? Why are you telling me I can't see my own friend?" I turned to the nurse. "Why is he here? Why can he tell me I can't go in?"

"He's here as a friend of the family," she said sympathetically, but not helpfully. "He is speaking for the family."

"The family doesn't want me out," I said to him. "Hector doesn't want me out. You're the only one who wants me out."

He spoke extra calm, the way he'd never speak to me in school if I was giving him lip. The way he surely wasn't going to speak to me the next time he caught me with no witnesses around. "Hector is not up to seeing his friends just now. When he is, we will let you know. Until then, please try to think of what's best for Hector."

He nodded at the nurse, nodded at me in a whole different way, and turned on his heel.

I looked to the nurse, who smiled like I was just a kid.

He was halfway down the bright white corridor when I started walking down there too. You could hear my school shoes all over the place because they were kind of cheap and very hard clopping off the tile floor. No matter how long I wore them they never got broken in. Skitz had his flimsy worn cordovans on, so he was silent like one of the nurses walking.

"How many aspirins did he eat, Father?" I asked. "Did he eat, like, hundreds of them? Thousands? Was he killing his really bad headache? Or maybe his really bad headache was killing *him*."

He kept walking silently, his hunchy black back standing out against everything else around.

He blurted, "You need to learn to mind your business, Mr. St. Cyr."

"That's just what I'm doing. I'm saying this is my business."

Shenanigan stopped short, spun around. I kept walking until I was just a couple of feet away from him. His eyes were scorching me.

"Is that so?"

I could feel Skitz tucked in close behind me, like I was behind him in the confessional. And just as good and quiet.

"That is so, Father," I said. I was hoping I sounded a lot less trembly on the outside than I felt on the inside. "We're a tribe, me and my pals. We always watch out for each other. We always watch. And when one of us falls, the other guys never leave him behind. We wait for him."

Father Shenanigan stood in front of me tensed up, straight rigid and glowing like a bottle rocket. His slicked hair was shinier in the hard hospital-corridor light, his bones sharper, his mustache broader and blacker. He looked like he knew exactly how frightening a person he was. He looked like he counted on it.

But he did not have anything to say. He turned on his heels again, and as he walked the last few feet to the door that had Hector Fossas's name handwritten on the sheet, Skitz Fitsimmons and I walked along too, my school shoes clip-clopping forcefully.

He turned on me with his hand on the door.

"What are you doing?" he snarled.

"I told you we came here to see our friend. I know he'll be glad to see us."

"And I told you, you cannot see him now."

Directly across from Hector's door, against the wall, was a molded plastic orange chair. I walked over and sat in it. Hands flat on my knees, in my white shirt and tie, I looked very smart and proper, I thought. Skitz, noticing there was no other chair, wedged in uncomfortably next to me.

"We'll wait," I said, firm, but I think I had my politeness back.

Father smacked the door hard with the heel of his

hand as he pushed his way into the room. "You may have a very long wait," he snapped.

You can't let your tribe down, no matter what. You can't turn your back and you can't do nothing. If you do, you're as bad as the rest of them.

"Okay," I said. "We'll be here."

"We'll be here," Skitz said. "Maybe not in the same chair, but we'll be here."

And we were. There every day at the hospital. And every day after the hospital. Every day, everywhere, all of us, always.